LA GUERRE, YES SIR!

Also by Roch Carrier

Jolis deuils (Editions du jour)
Contes pour mille oreilles (Ecrits du Canada Français)
Floralie, où es-tu? (Editions du jour)
Il est par là, le soleil (Editions du jour)

LA GUERRE, YES SIR!

ROCH CARRIER

TRANSLATED BY SHEILA FISCHMAN

Published by
House of Anansi Press Limited
1800 Steeles Avenue West
Concord, Ontario
L4K 2P3

Reprinted August 1993

First English edition published in 1970 by
House of Anansi Press Limited

Published in French in 1968 by
Editions du Jour
1651, rue Saint-Denis
Montreal, Canada

Canadian Cataloguing in Publication Data

Carrier, Roch, 1937-
La guerre, yes Sir!

ISBN 0-88784-515-0

I. Title.

PS8505.A77G813 1991   C843'.54   C70-3937

Cover design: Brant Cowie/ArtPlus Limited
Printed and bound in Canada

I dedicate this book, which I have dreamed,
to those who have perhaps lived it.

. *R.C.*

The translation is for my teacher, T.J. Casaubon.

S.F.

The reader may be surprised to see words, phrases and even whole sentences left in the original French. The title, to begin with. Although a literal translation would have been simple enough, The War, Oui Monsieur! *just doesn't have the same force, and Roch Carrier's brilliant title is a succinct comment on the English—French situation in Quebec, particularly as it existed during the second World War.*

The swearing has also been left in French. Aside from the war and the conflicts that arose from it, the relationship of the villagers to the Church is perhaps the novel's single most important theme. The people are unquestioning Catholics, faithful churchgoers, for whom the parish priest is the most influential person in the community. The relationship is not always a happy one, though, and there is an underlying resentment of it, a desire to escape in some way from its strictures. This rebellion is achieved in a figurative way by the use of a most amazing collection of oaths and curses, which call on virtually every object of religious significance to Roman

1

Catholics, from the wood of the Crucifix to the chrism (Saint Chrême) or sacred oil. These words, uttered in despair or grief or anger — or sometimes in affection — have the same emotional force as some of the Anglo-Saxon expletives. To translate them thus, however, would have been to distort the values of the people who use them; on the other hand, literal translations would have been at best perplexing, more often simply absurd. A "chalice of a host of a tabernacle" just doesn't produce the effect of "calice d'hostie de tabernacle" — pronounced calisse and tabarnaque. "Maudits Anglais" — goddamn Englishmen — is probably only too familiar already.

In a way, the people who used these oaths literally to challenge the Church's authority could be considered the first Quebec revolutionaries; now, of course, the words have lost their strength and revolutionaries have other tactics, other targets.

Then there are the prayers. The villagers' unquestioning attendance at Mass and their observance of the rituals does not preclude an ignorance of what the formulas they faithfully repeat are all about. The result is some marvellously mangled prayers, even the most familiar, that are, unfortunately, completely untranslatable. James Joyce did something similar in his "Hail Mary full of grease, the lard is with you."

A brief glossary may be helpful. "Christ," pronounced "crisse," is one of the strongest expletives; others include "hostie" (host), "ciboire" (ciborium), Crucifix, "Vierge" (the Blessed Virgin), "baptême" (baptism). Nor is the Pope spared.

Anyway, whatever the results of attempts to make Canada officially bilingual, a little personal bilingualism never hurt anybody. Learning to swear in the other language may be an unorthodox way to begin, but it could stir up some interest. And create some understanding that might even help to eliminate one of the most frequently used expressions — "maudits Anglais."

S.F.

Joseph wasn't panting.

He approached like a man walking to work. Which hand would he put on the log, his right hand or his left? His right hand was stronger, better for working. His left hand was strong too.

Joseph spread the five fingers of his left hand on the log.

He heard breathing behind him. He turned around. It was his own.

His other fingers, his other hand, seized the axe. It crashed down between the wrist and the hand, which leapt into the snow and was slowly drowned in his blood.

Joseph did not see the red stain or the hand or the snow. When the axe cut through the bone Joseph felt only a warm caress; his suffering began when it was buried in the wood. The cloudy window separating him from life gradually became very clear, transparent. In a moment of dizzy lucidity Joseph was aware of the fear that had tortured him for long months:

"Their Christly shells would have made jam out of me . . . " He drove his stump into the snow. "They've already made jam out of Corriveau with their goddamn war . . . They won't get me . . . me, I'll be making jam next fall: strawberries, blueberries, gooseberries, red apples, raspberries . . . "

Joseph burst into a great laugh, which he could hear going up very high, up above the snow. He hadn't had so much fun since the beginning of the war. The villagers heard his voice. He was calling for help.

★ ★ ★ ★ ★

Amélie rapped on the ceiling with the handle of her broom. It was code. She listened. There was a whispering movement in the attic: a man accustomed to moving around silently. Nothing stirred. Then a mewing sound could be distinguished. That meant: "Is it dangerous? "

Then Amélie called out, "Come on down, gutless! "

Some heavy objects slid, a trap door opened in the ceiling, a boot appeared, then the other, and the legs. Arthur let himself down, a rifle in his hand, a coat folded under his arm.

"No, you don't need all that stuff . . . Come and get into bed," Amélie ordered.

Arthur turned around, looking for a spot to lay down his things.

"Come to bed Arthur," Amélie insisted. "Hurry up. Men! They've got their feet stuck in molasses. I can't figure out why we need them so badly. Arthur, throw your package in the corner and come to bed."

Another head appeared in the opening. Henri.

"It was my turn to sleep with you tonight," he muttered.

"You," she flung the words at him, "shut up! The kids can't get to sleep."

"It's my turn tonight."

"You'll get your turn. Go and hide."

6

"It's never my turn," Henri protested. "Are you my wife or aren't you? "

Amélie planted herself in the trap-door of the attic, her hands on her hips, and started spitting out insults. Henri heard nothing. He was dazzled by the swelling breasts he could see in the neckline of her dress.

"Yes, I'm your wife," Amélie assured him, "but if I wasn't Arthur's woman too I wouldn't have had kids by him."

"There's no more justice," Henri wept. "Ever since this goddam war started there's been no justice."

Henri had been obliged to dress himself up like a soldier. He had been pushed into a boat, and let out in England.

"What's England? " the gossips used to ask Amélie, who was more than a little proud to have her husband a soldier in England. "England, it's one of the old countries. First there's the sea. The sea is as big as the world. On the other side, there's England. It's at the end of the world, England is. It's a long way away. You can't even go there by train. Oh yes, my Henri is in England. He's fighting the Germans. Then when there aren't any more Germans Henri sweeps the army's floor, in England."

This was how she used to interpret Henri's letters. But with her feminine intuition she knew that Henri was spending his time in England drinking and stroking women's behinds.

"A man on his own," she used to think, "is a tomcat, and besides in those old countries they don't have any morals or religion . . . "

In her prayers Amélie often used to ask the good Lord that if Henri got himself killed by a German his soul wouldn't be dirty like his boots. The good Lord couldn't

7

refuse her that.

Henri had been gone for more than a year. One night someone knocked at her door. Amélie, worried, hesitated to open it. You don't knock at night on the door of the wife of a soldier at the front in England without a very serious motive. Finally Amélie decided to open the latch. It was Arthur, his rifle in his hand.

"Don't kill me," she pleaded, closing the neckline of her dress, which scarcely contained her bosom.

Arthur stared for a moment at the closed hand and the swelling dress. "I want to hide. Hide me."

Amélie stepped aside to let him in.

"Is it on account of the war? If it goes on very long all the women are going to have a man hidden under their skirts."

Arthur laughed. "The military police have got their dogs on my trail. They came to my place, the cops and the dogs. I ducked out the door. I killed one of the dogs. I don't want to go to their goddam war."

"Henri's at the war . . . "

"I don't want to get my face torn up in their goddamn war. Did they ask us if we wanted this goddamn war? No. But when they need men to fight, then they like us well enough. As far as I'm concerned I'm not going to lose a single hair in their goddamn war.

It seemed to Amélie that Arthur was much more right than Henri. Her husband always let himself be taken in by someone or something.

"I don't want to go to their war. The big guys have decided to make their war. Let them do it alone, without us. Let the big guys fight each other if that's what they want; it doesn't hurt them. They always start again. Let them have fun, but let the little guys enjoy themselves the way they want."

Amélie agreed. Arthur was right, Henri was wrong. "It's the end of the world."

"My God, is it possible? "

"Yes, Madame."

"My God," sighed Amélie, raising her arms in a gesture of supplication. A breast popped out of her open dress. Amélie pushed it inside. "You'll sleep in the attic," she said.

Arthur slept in Amélie's bed. When they woke up at dawn she said to him, "There are cows to milk."

"That's my job."

Arthur got up, got dressed, and on his way out took Henri's jacket which was hanging up near the door. He came back with the milk.

"Those cows were sure glad to see a man."

"How about me; you think I wasn't glad too? "

The children came and sat around the table, and Arthur talked to them about the war that was killing little children, about the Germans who were cutting little children into pieces to feed to their dogs.

The cross-eyed child said, "If a German comes here I'm going to stick my fork in his eye."

"I," said a little girl, "am going to throw a stone at his glasses and the glass will bust his eyes open."

The eldest said, "I'm going to put a snake in a glass of milk and he'll drink the snake."

"I'm going to war like my father," said the youngest.

"Shut up, all of you," Amélie interrupted. "Just be happy you've got something to eat."

"I don't like the war," Arthur explained, "because in a war little children are killed; I don't want little children to be killed." With these words Arthur became the child-

9

ren's father.

Amélie beamed with joy. Henri, their real father, had never known how to talk to the children. Arthur, a bachelor, did. No one thought he should leave. One morning nine months later the children found, in the little bed, two twins, crying and hungry. Amélie laughed happily. "The others are more mine than yours, but the twins are ours."

Arthur kept busy with the chores and the animals; he was never completely free, however, but always afraid that the army dogs would leap on his back. The farm was no longer abandoned. Amélie spoiled Arthur like a favourite child.

One evening Henri appeared in the doorway.

"It's about time you came back," Amélie commented. "We were starting to forget you."

"I've only come for a few days. I've got to go back."

"Why did they send you back here? "

"I was tired. The war wears you out."

"Who's going to fight the Germans while you're here? "

Henri dropped into a chair. "It's tiring, the war."

"You think I'm not tired too, when you've left me here with the kids? Everybody's tired. The twins wear me out, but you don't hear me complain about being tired."

"The twins? "

"Yes, the twins."

Henri didn't understand at all. At the war he had often thought of his children. How could he forget a pair of twins? Perhaps they had been very young when he left. He couldn't have forgotten that he had twins. A man who has twins doesn't forget them.

"Twins," explained Amélie. "Two sets of twins. I

have two sets of twin boys. Because the gentleman travels, because the gentleman goes for walks, because the gentleman thinks he's obliged to go off to war, the gentleman thinks the earth stops turning. I've got twins; two sets of twin boys. It's simple. I lugged them around in there," she tapped her belly, "and then they came out."

"What interests me is how they got in."

"I've got twins," she cut in finally, "and they're alive and well."

That evening they bickered, they fought, they swatted the whimpering children, they kicked and punched. When they were worn out they made peace.

After his long absence Henri deserved to be well received. Henri, then, would sleep with his wife. In the future, both Henri and Arthur would have their rights in turn, for as long as the soldier was on leave.

On the last day of his holiday Henri refused to leave Amélie to go back to the war.

"Two men in a house is too much for one woman," Amélie insisted. "There's a war. Somebody's got to do it. There have to be men at the war and men in the house. All the men can't stay at home. Some of them have got to go away. The bravest ones become soldiers and go away to fight."

Arthur added his arguments in a reproachful tone. "The Germans will come along with those boots of theirs that fall on the floor like the blows of an axe and you, you want to stay here and smoke your pipe."

Henri banged his fists on the table; children were crying everywhere in the house. "You," he shouted, "you, are you going to war?"

Arthur lit his pipe and answered calmly, through the smoke. "You're a soldier . . . "

"Germans! I've never seen an *hostie* of a German."

"You're a soldier; you've got the uniform, you've got the boots. Me, I'm a farmer and the father of a family. I've got two sets of twins and Amélie's expecting again. You're a soldier. Soldiers have a duty to protect farmers who are fathers of families, and the children and the cattle and the country."

Henri didn't go back to the front.

"Since this *tabernacle* of a war there's been no more justice," he whined, his head hanging in the opening of the trap-door. "It's never my turn. I should have ended up like Corriveau. Corriveau doesn't see anything any more."

"You're men," said Amélie with a purr in her voice, "and you've got to behave like men and not like children. Listen to each other peacefully. It's not worth it for you two to fight about it — both of you gets his turn in my bed, that's the rule. It's not hard to understand. Each one has his rights. I can't always know whose turn it is. I can't always know if it was Henri who was with me yesterday or Arthur. Shut the trapdoor, Henri, and don't make any more noise. You know they're looking for deserters, and they find the ones that make too much noise."

She grabbed Arthur by the arm.

"Come on. When you get right down to it it's not much fun for my poor Henri. He'd like to spend days in my bed. It's tough, the war."

With his eyes Henri followed his wife and Arthur until they had disappeared into the bedroom.

"Calice d'hostie de tabernacle! I'll be glad when this war is over . . ."

He closed the trapdoor and slid some heavy objects over it.

Turning her back to Arthur, Amélie unbuttoned her

12

dress. Arthur watched her. He resisted the desire to leap onto her and crush her breasts in his hands. She let her dress fall; the soft flesh of her back and hips, white and gleaming, blinded Arthur. That back: he could never get used to it. She bent down to take off her pants which she let fall against her legs. Then she turned towards Arthur. He was trembling at the realization that he was about to make his nest in that flesh.

"Corriveau arrives tomorrow," she said.

She fell onto the bed without drawing back the covers.

"Hurry up," she said, "I'm cold. Hear the wind? It's sad, a winter wind. Come on, hurry up."

Arthur stretched out on the bed. "I forgot that Corriveau was coming tomorrow. He'll have soldiers with him, so Henri and I can't take a chance and leave the house. Corriveau's going to bust his gut laughing in his coffin."

He felt the generous flesh with rapture. Amélie chuckled. But the fingers loosened. The hand was not ravenous. It fell back on the sheet.

"Corriveau was away for three years," he said. "I remember, it was the beginning of fall. He didn't think he'd be away for long."

"Yeah, and he didn't think he wouldn't be coming back."

"Oh, I don't know if he wanted to come back. The last word he said, I remember as if it was yesterday, he said, 'At last I'm going to have some peace.' He said that. I can still hear it."

"In war, time must pass quickly," she said.

Arthur's sex was too pacific.

"To be away for three years and come back in your

13

coffin, that's no life. Whether you've got a cortège of soldiers or not."

"Dying," murmured Amélie, "that's sad."

"Dying in a war is sad all right."

"Poor Corriveau."

Amélie had rolled onto Arthur; feeling trapped by the heavy breasts and the burning belly, he got out of the bed, picked up his clothes, grabbed the broom, and knocked on the ceiling according to the agreement. The heavy objects slid in the attic, the trapdoor opened, and Henri's head appeared. He yelled, "You can't even sleep around here! They steal your lawful wife who's been blessed by the priest and then they disturb you three or four times a night and just as often in the day. Peace! I want some peace, *hostie*! "

Arthur waited for a moment's silence so that he could talk. It came. "It's sad to come back from the war in your coffin."

"It's sad, but it's no reason to disturb the whole village."

"For me it stirs up my soul, my heart, my liver, my guts, that Corriveau is dead."

"Stir up whatever you want, that won't bring him back."

"It's sad; he was our age."

"He was younger than us," Henri corrected.

"Dying: I couldn't stand that."

"What's wrong with you, stomping around under my trapdoor like a cat pissing in the bran? "

"I'm coming up to the attic. If you want, Henri, you can take my place."

"Okay."

"Take my turn tonight," Arthur went on. "But tomorrow's mine."

14

★ ★ ★ ★ ★

The scalded pig, all open, the inside of the body a bright red, had its two back legs tied to the ladder on which Arsène had stretched it out. The oldest of his fourteen children, who knew this kind of work well, took hold of one of the animal's front feet and stretched it with all his might, his foot supported on a rung of the ladder. When the beast was sufficiently extended he tied the foot to a rung and seized the fourth foot to begin the same operation over again. Then Arsène and his son lifted the ladder so that it was vertical and leaned it against a wall of the barn. The youth contemplated the skinned pig, the inside of the animal like an immense red wound.

"Every time I see a pig laid out like that I can't help thinking of Christ on Calvary."

"Philibert!" his father yelled. "Atheist! You'll be damned! Ask the good Lord's pardon right now and come here so I can give you a boot in the ass!"

Philibert, his eyes fixed on the opened pig, didn't move a hair. His father came up to him, grumbling that he was a damn blasphemer, that he would bring down misfortunes on the house, such as foot-and-mouth disease, thunder, cancer, debts, and hunch-backed children.

"Every time somebody insults Christ, the pope and holy things, he pays for it," explained Arsène.

He would have liked his son to understand, but he knew that gentleness is never effective. So he buried his boot in Philibert's behind and repeated the action until his leg was tired.

Tears flowed from Philibert's eyes. Was this what life was all about? Was this why a child was supposed to

15

honour his father all the days of his life? Philibert had no desire to honour his father. He wouldn't honour him to the end of his days. He'd go away soon like all the boys in the village. The young boys left the village because they had no intention of honouring their fathers to the end of their days. Philibert knew what he wanted to be when the day came for him to leave . . . And he wouldn't come back before he'd forgotten the kicks he had received. These kicks, he thought, should never be forgotten, so maybe he'd never come back.

"You're a kid with one hell of a mouth; you're possessed by the devil, my boy, the living devil. May God protect me, his father, from eternal damnation."

Arsène gave Philibert his most powerful kick.

"It's not worth killing me," said Philibert craftily. "I didn't mean anything bad. I just meant that Christ must have suffered a lot, stretched out on his cross like that pig."

Arsène replied with another kick. Philibert pursued his idea. "Getting stuck on a cross and having knives stuck in your belly, that can't be very much fun."

"You're still blaspheming! Are you dead set on making hell come down on us like a rain of fire? "

Arsène hit his resigned son several times. Then he calmed down. A long silence paralysed them. Father and son were back to back; they remained motionless for some time, not daring to let out the insults they exchanged internally, silently. Arsène resolved to speak. He couldn't be silent till the end of the world.

"You know, my boy, that punishment on the cross is still practised today. And it must be more painful today than in the olden days because nowadays our flesh isn't so tough."

Philibert had nothing to say.

"The Germans are still putting prisoners on the cross," Arsène went on.

"I'd sure like to see a German. I'd see how it's done and then I'd kill him."

"The Germans put women on the cross."

"Why not men? "

"The Germans prefer women on the cross. With men they couldn't do the same thing."

"Because the men would bust their teeth."

"I think I can tell you now, you're big enough to understand. I was telling you that the Germans stretch the women out on crosses . . . "

"Yes, you told me that."

"Women are women, but the crosses aren't crosses . . . "

"Ah! "

"The crosses are beds."

Philibert looked at his father wide-eyed with astonishment.

"The Germans get on top of the woman attached to the bed one after another, and then they take advantage of her till she's dead."

"What do the Germans do to the woman? "

"Nitwit! " cried Arsène, booting him in the rear.

The child suddenly caught on. "Did Corriveau do that too? "

Arsène looked at his son indulgently. "What am I going to do with you? I'm trying to educate you and then, *Sainte Vierge*, you refuse to understand a thing. Are you a birdbrain? Corriveau didn't do that. Corriveau isn't a German. Our soldiers don't behave like Germans. Our soldiers fight clean," explained Arsène; "they defend our

17

rights, our religion, our animals, everything that belongs to us."

When would Philibert be able to go to war with the Germans, kill a German?

"Did Corriveau knock down any Germans? "

"Today they kill without seeing each other, and without seeing each other they die. Anyway, even if he did see any, Corriveau won't be able to tell us now."

★ ★ ★ ★ ★

Joseph appeared, his arm wrapped up in rags soaked in alcohol and red with blood that was beginning to harden because of the cold.

"It's the Anglais, that's for sure, that are coming with Corriveau," he announced. "The army told Anthyme Corriveau. There'll be seven. Seven Anglais."

"Anthyme was right to buy a whole pig from me," Arsène noted.

"There'll be seven of them."

"That'll make a lot of people trying to find a hair on my pig."

"There'll be seven Anglais, seven soldiers. That means that six are going to carry Corriveau, three on each side. The seventh is the most important. He gives the orders. A soldier doesn't do a thing, he doesn't even fart without an order."

Philibert was amazed.

"I can't wait to see these Anglais; I've never seen

18

one."

Arsène looked at him in the manner of a man who knows everything. "The Anglais, my boy, are like everybody else. The men pee standing up and the women do it sitting down."

He held out a bucket to the boy. "Go ask your mother if she has some boiling water. There can't be a single *hostie* of a bristle on this pig. Hurry up! "

Philibert ran towards the house, the bucket in his hand, thinking of the insulting things he could say to the real Anglais. Arsène noticed some blood on Joseph's bandages.

"What's the matter, Joseph my friend, did you scratch yourself? "

Bralington Station.

The train could be seen in the distance, the engine ploughing through the snow covering the forest. At the station you couldn't see it approaching, there was so much frost on the windows. You could only tell it was coming by the noise. The stationmaster withdrew into the shed, sliding the door on its rusted pulleys so that the employees could unload the merchandise there. In his little station, smelling of charcoal and the loafers' tobacco, the station agent had forgotten about all the snow.

He swore, "May God change my mother into a horse with the head of a cow if I've ever seen so much snow in my life. And I've seen some."

"Snow," said the storekeeper. "There's more snow than there are *hosties* in all the *tabernacles*. This morning I want to go out the door, like a gentleman. So I can't even open it! It was blocked by the snow. Hard snow, like ice. Okay, so I climb up the stairs, I open a window, and I go out the window like a *ciboire* of a savage."

"I used to be in the Royal Navy," said the stationmaster. "The first time I found myself in front of the ocean I said to myself, I said: 'Open your eyes. By Christ, you've never seen so much water all at once.' "

"Me, I don't like water. A glass of water makes me seasick. Goddamn water. There's only one way not to make me seasick: put alcohol in my water."

"Okay," continued the stationmaster, who had not lost his train of thought, "today when I saw all that snow I said to myself, 'Open your eyes, grandpa, you've never seen so much snow.' "

"You can't please everybody, but the polar bears must be pretty happy."

The conductor loomed into sight in a cloud of snow, as though blown by a gust of wind. In his hand he held a watch that was attached to his stomach by a little chain, and he watched it beat as if it were his heart. "With all this snow," he said, "you don't move very fast. We're behind two hours, seventeen minutes and forty-four seconds."

"With all this snow," repeated the stationmaster, "there's a danger that polar bears will come down from the North. It's been known to happen: polar bears have come down into the villages. Because of the snow they thought they were on home ground. In cases like that they devour everybody in the village. Polar bears never have indiges-

20

tion. When I was sailing in the navy . . ."

The conductor didn't have time to listen to another fragment of the stationmaster's autobiography. "We're late," he interrupted. "At every station everybody has to work faster: the time lost by the train has to be made up by men."

Storekeepers were bringing down cases and packages. The stationmaster checked to see that they were in good condition, to make sure that the fastening had not been broken or the wrapping undone during the trip. As each object was inspected he made a little mark on a list that he brought up close to his nose so he could read it.

"Eaton's? OK. Mont-Rouge? OK. Brunswick? OK. Montreal Shipping? OK. Clark Beans? OK. Marini Spaghetti? OK. Black and White? OK. Black Horse? OK. William Scotch? OK. 1, 2, 3, 4, 5, 6, 7, . . . Corriveau? Corriveau? " he shouted. "Corriveau? Where have you put Corriveau? "

"Corriveau? " somebody asked from the inside of the car, "What's that, Corriveau? "

"Corriveau's a coffin."

The voice in the car gave an order. "The dead guy gets off here. Where did you put the dead guy? "

"Are you going to let him off? " asked the stationmaster impatiently.

"He isn't here now," said the voice in the car. "He must have got off to stretch his legs."

"He should have better come and help me shovel," said an employee who was trying to clear the platform.

"That *baptême* of a corpse, he isn't there," complained the voice in the car. "There's always trouble with these dead guys. I'd rather ship ten living men than one dead one."

The stationmaster's voice took on the dry tone of

21

someone in authority. "Friends, I don't want you to make a mistake with that package. Corriveau is one of us. He's going to get off here. I want Corriveau to get off with his Anglais."

"Ah! " sighed the man inside, relieved. "I get it. If you're talking about the Anglais, all their baggage is off."

The man appeared in the door of the car, triumphant. The stationmaster marked his sheet in the necessary place and went back into his office.

Through his wicket he noticed the képis of some soldiers who were sitting in the waiting room. "Hey! boys," he asked, "did you get a nice trip? "

"Not too lovely, monsieur," one of the soldiers replied in French.

"I understand English, boys. You may speak English. I learned when I was in the navy – Royal Navy."

"All the peoples speaks English," said the same soldier, still speaking French.

"Where is Corriveau? "

"What means Corllivouuw? "

"Corriveau is the name of our poor boy, boys."

"The man is in there," said one of the soldiers, indicating the coffin on which they were sitting and smoking cigarettes.

The one who was the leader got up; with a single military movement the other six soldiers took up their positions. Then they gave the stationmaster a military salute and carried away the coffin, leaving the waiting-room door open to the cold.

The stationmaster grumbled: "You can see these *maudits* Anglais are used to having niggers or French Canadians to shut their doors. That's what Corriveau must have done: open and shut doors for the Anglais."

22

A thin man, an employee who had finished his work, was going from one window to another as though he were looking for something important. He wasn't discouraged although he kept running into opaque frost. He walked as though he knew where he was going. The man pulled his finger out of his nostril. "Life," he declared, "is nothing but this: there's the big guys and the little guys. There's the good Lord and there's me. There's the Germans and there was Corriveau. There's the Anglais and us; you, Corriveau, me, everybody in the village . . ."

The man plunged his finger back into the nostril, where it had lots to do.

"Corriveau," said the stationmaster "is the first child the war has taken from us."

The man removed his finger from his nose and pointed it accusingly towards the stationmaster. "You mean Corriveau is the first child the big guys have grabbed away from us. Shit on the big guys. They're all the same: Germans, Anglais, French, Russians, Chinese, Japs; they're all so much alike they have to wear different costumes to tell each other apart before they throw their grenades. I shit on all the big guys, but not on the good Lord, because he's even bigger than the big guys. But he's a big guy too. They're all big guys. That's why I think this war, it's a war of the big guys against the little ones. Corriveau's dead. The little guys are dying. The big guys last forever."

The man stuck his finger back in his nose and began again his promenade from one window to another, all of them covered with frost.

The stationmaster lit his pipe. "If Corriveau had died here, in the village, in his bed, that would have been very sad for a young man. But he died in his soldier suit and far away from the village; that must mean something."

"That means that the big guys get bigger and the little ones go bust."

23

★ ★ ★ ★ ★

Madame Joseph wished she were a dog. With sharp claws and furious barks she would have chased, dispersed and bitten the legs of the gang of urchins blocking her way.

Madame Joseph was going back to her house. She could not endure, on her own, the pain of becoming the wife of a man who had chopped off his own hand with an axe. She had gone to tell her neighbours about her troubles. "Life is hard," she had said, tears in her eyes. "You marry a man and you find out you're sleeping with an invalid. What's Joseph going to do with his stump in my bed?"

It was a sad story indeed. The neighbours, helpless before her misfortune, all promised to pray for her and Joseph. In any case it was not certain whether Josph had done wrong, because it said in the Gospel, "Tear out thy hand or throw it on the fire." Because that was truly said in the Gospel, Madame Joseph was almost consoled.

She returned, then, along the snowy path dug in the piled-up snow by the horses and villagers. She walked with as much dignity as possible because, behind the curtains, they were watching her; in the houses they were talking about her and Joseph.

The children in the street were too busy with their game to see her coming. Divided into two teams, everyone was armed with a curved stick as in a hockey game; they were fighting over an object, probably a frozen horse turd, trying to push it into the other side's goal. Sticks were raised and came crashing down; the players held on, knocked each other around, waved their sticks, banged them together with a dry sound. Suddenly the object shot outside the milling group; the players ran after it, tripped

24

each other, exchanged blows with their sticks, their elbows, got hold of it again, all the time shouting and swearing as the sticks came crashing down, clattering on one another. The object was rolling farther along on the snow again, among the shouts of joy and swearing of those who had scored a point.

Madame Joseph didn't dare go on. She couldn't attempt a detour off the road. She'd sink in the snow.

How would she manage to get by this horde? Would she shout, "Let me past?" They would leap on her; they would roll her in the snow and amuse themselves by looking at her thighs and seeing her pants. The thighs and pants of Madame Joseph were spots of great interest for the boys of the village. Other women could go along the road with no trouble, without being bothered, but as soon as Madame Joseph went out the boys invented a new way to get a look at her thighs.

"We hatch them and they turn out to be vicious little morons who will always prefer the bordellos to the Church," she thought, a little sadly. "There isn't one of those kids who isn't the spitting image of his father. We don't beat them enough."

With an instinctive movement she tightened her thighs and advanced cautiously.

Suddenly furious, she raised her arms and brought her fists down on the little boy closest to her. She grabbed hold of a stick, struck out at random, fiercely, shouting threats. "Little morons! vicious little monsters! damn brats! pigs! *I'll* show you how to play hockey!"

Madame Joseph grabbed a second stick, waved it around in front of her head, and struck out to the left, to the right, everywhere at once, in front, behind. Her sticks hit noses, ears, eyes, heads. The boys were soon dispersed. From a distance they shouted their insults: "Fat ass! Big tits! You've got the face of a cow walking backwards!

You look like a holy Virgin turned upside down! "

"Vicious little monsters! Damned brats! You're all set to visit the bordellos in town! "

They replied, "If we go to the bordellos we go to see your daughters! "

She stopped speaking their language. She could not insult them. They knew all the insults. "We don't beat them enough," she complained.

She got down on her knees and picked up the object they had been fighting over with their sticks — her husband's chopped-off hand. The fingers were closed and hard as a rock. There were black marks where their sticks had struck it. Madame Joseph put it in the pocket of her fur coat and went back to her house, announcing to the boys, who were choking with laughter, that the devil would punish them in hell.

Joseph was sitting in his chair, pale, with a tortured face.

"I've found your hand, Joseph."

He looked at her indifferently.

"It's a good thing I went that way; the kids were playing hockey with your hand."

Joseph said nothing.

"If I hadn't got there in time the brats would have broken it. You should thank me."

Bored by his wife's insistence he finally answered. "What do you want to do with my hand? Make soup? "

"You're a lazy good-for-nothing."

Joseph looked at his wife sadly. "Apparently Corriveau's arrived at the station."

Waving his battered arm, all covered with bloody rags, he exclaimed, "Now let them come and take me off to fight their Christly war! I'll cut off their dinks, if they've got any. I'll cut them off like I cut off my hand. I'm not going to fight their goddamn war."

Madame Joseph whistled between her teeth at the dog, who woke up and obeyed her call. She threw the hand out the door into the snow. The dog ran after it, growling with pleasure.

"You think it makes me happy to sleep with a man who's only got one hand . . ."

"I always thought you'd have liked to see me go off to the war and you wouldn't have minded too much if I'd come back like Corriveau. At a certain age all women want to be widows."

Madame Joseph stood in front of her husband, her hands on her hips, and spoke to him as though she were spitting in his face. "A man who doesn't have the courage to go and fight a war to protect his country is no man. You'd let the Germans walk all over you. You're not a man. I wonder what I'm sleeping with."

Joseph murmured gently between his teeth. "Corriveau? Is Corriveau a man? "

★ ★ ★ ★ ★

The road between the village and the station had disappeared in the snow like a stream in a white, blinding flood. No one lived here. No house. The forest was weighted down by the snow, which spread out as far as the eye could see, sparkling in all its dunes, its rises, its very shadows; because of the snow it seemed no longer alive, but a mute white plaster.

On the other side of the endless forest the snow continued to the horizon.

How could they have got away, these men who were bent under a coffin and sinking into the snow up to their belts? They were six soldiers carrying the burden, three on each side, and in front of them a sergeant shouted to make them go on. Each step required an effort. First they had to lift a leg out of the snow, which gripped the foot with a strong suction, then raise the foot as high as possible without losing balance, stretch the leg then, and push the foot energetically, press it into the snow until it was hard, still without losing balance, and without moving the coffin too much, because all the weight carried by one man would be transferred to the shoulders of another; they had to hurry. It was already later than they had expected. The sergeant was in a bad mood. He nagged his men, who were sweating in this plain of snow, under the coffin they were carrying on their shoulders from the station to the village. It was not the first coffin they had carried, but they had never gone as far as they had that day, and at each step the village on the mountain seemed farther away, as though they had changed directions in the snow.

The soldiers were sweating. Their clothes were soaked. The sweat rolled down their backs in cold globules. Sweat poured onto their faces too, and froze after sitting motionless on their chins; they could feel the skin growing stiff. Their swollen lips had slowly become paralyzed. They didn't dare to say a word, to swear or laugh or

28

complain, they were so close to the breaking point. Their wet hair was steaming. The cold stung their hands like spiny bushes.

The soldiers didn't even suspect that there was a road hidden under the snow. They simply walked on like animals. They went on towards the mountains where they saw chimneys above the snow, their smoke like a comforting balm to the men. In the silence, where nothing vibrated but the effort of their breathing, they remembered, bent down under their fatigue, their own houses which they hadn't seen for months.

With no order from the sergeant, with a spontaneous gesture, they lowered the coffin from their shoulders and put it down.

"I'm dead hungry," said one.

They took up their burden again and continued on in the snow.

★ ★ ★ ★ ★

Busy surveying the unloading of merchandise, the station master had not seen the soldier Bérubé get off the train, accompanied by his wife, Molly, whom he was bringing home from Newfoundland. What a surprise this arrival would be. He had not warned his family, either that he was coming home or that he had recently been married. His letters didn't say a thing.

Basically, Bérubé had only one topic to write about: that he could tell nothing about his life as a soldier, or

29

about the war, and that he didn't know what would happen to him tomorrow. He kept himself ready for everything, he wrote. His mother couldn't read a line without bursting into sobs: how painful this war was, when a son couldn't tell his mother about his life.

Bérubé was responsible for looking after the toilets in G wing of B building at the airforce base in Gander, Newfoundland. Bérubé had learned to speak English. He spoke it as well as all the other toilet-cleaners, whether they were Poles, Italians, Hungarians or Greeks.

Waiting for the plane that would take him to Montreal, where he would catch a train, Bérubé decided to stay at the Aviator Hotel. Before he had even ordered a drink at the bar a soft hand stroked him, and an insinuating English voice said, "Come with me, darling."

"Darling?"

"Come . . ."

"Where are you going, by the way?"

"To my bedroom."

"OK, let's go!"

Bérubé followed the girl. As he watched her walking ahead of him, her hips swaying in her narrow skirt, and as he speculated about the well-formed behind, Bérubé's legs felt numb; the rug in the corridor became rough and lumpy for him. He had the feeling that each of the girl's steps and each movement of her body tightened invisible ties around him. He hurried, because she was walking quickly. When he put a hand on her behind and she did not take it away his disagreeable paralysis dissolved and he was suddenly sure of himself and even a little cold.

"Tu es un bien beau bébé, chérie."

"What did you say?"

"Be a good girl."

30

The girl turned towards him and, laughing, stuck out her tongue and pushed away his hand. She opened the door of her room. "Shut the door behind you!" she ordered. Then, making her voice more caressing, she said, "Give me five dollars. Take off your clothes."

Bérubé feverishly tore off his tunic and sat on the bed to undo his shirt. He was trembling; he had the feeling that the bed was charged with electricity. He undid his fly and took off his trousers, which he threw onto a chair. He turned his head towards Molly. What kind of modesty was making her turn her back as she undressed? Bérubé wanted to see a naked girl.

"Hey! look at me," he said.

Bérubé felt it was ridiculous to be sitting on a bed when a girl was getting undressed on the other side, but he didn't dare stand up: the girl would make fun of what had happened to him. He remained seated and blushed.

"Come, darling."

The girl was before him, naked. She had kept on her brassiere, which was full to bursting. She held out her arms to Bérubé who was incapable of getting up, of leaping towards the naked girl, of seizing her in his arms, of clutching her violently and throwing her on the bed. Bérubé felt completely weak, as if he had had too much to drink. In his head he heard a tick-tock like a drumbeat. "Always, never," repeated the monstrous clock which had marked the hours of his childhood, the clock of hell which throughout eternity would say "always, never"; the damned are in hell for ever, they never leave. "Always, never." Under the clock Bérubé saw the viscous caverns of hell where serpents climbed, mingled with the eternal flames. And he saw the damned — naked, strangling in the flames — and the serpents. "Always, never": the clock of his childhood beat out the measure, the clock of eternal damnation for those who go naked and those who touch naked women; "always, never," sounded the clock and Bérubé had to beg, "Do you want to marry me? "

"Yes," replied the girl, who had never been asked this question.

"What's your name? "

"Molly."

"Oh! Molly, I want you to be mine," said Bérubé, getting up and going towards her.

They embraced. Molly let herself fall onto the bed, and the marriage was celebrated.

Then they got dressed again. Bérubé took her in a taxi to the Padré, to confess and receive the sacrament. The Padré did not hesitate to give his blessing.

Before they took the plane to Montreal Bérubé and Molly went to buy a wedding dress, which she insisted on putting on right away.

★ ★ ★ ★ ★

Molly was shivering in her long bouffant white gown, which the wind was trying to snatch away from her. Neither the horse-drawn carriages nor the snowmobiles had been able to get to the station to pick up the travellers. Bérubé said simply, "Molly, climb up on my shoulders. Get on my back, we'll take our bags another day."

They started to go up towards the village. Bérubé powerfully dug a passage through the snow, which came up to his chest. Because of the white lace tickling his face and because of Molly's warm thighs which were pressed tightly against his cheeks, Bérubé felt a desire to toss her into the snow and leap onto her, but that would have rumpled her dress and made Molly all snowy; when they arrived at the village people would soon guess what had gone on and they would be amused at Bérubé's impatience.

This way, in the snow, Bérubé tried to think of nothing in order not to think of Molly's thighs, of her breasts, bigger than fine apples, of her buttocks beneath the white dress. But it was impossible to think of nothing; one always has a picture inside one's head, or a sensation, or the memory of a picture of a sensation, or even a desire. A feeling of warmth, the good warmth of Molly's thighs, of her belly, of the warmth between her breasts, clouded Bérubé's thoughts, threw into his head and before his eyes a fog that dazed him. He did not know if he was still going in the right direction; he could no longer see the village on the mountain, and the snow was as deep as the sea. Bérubé could think of nothing but the warmth of Molly, and this warmth moved over his body like a caressing hand, so that even the snow pressing against his legs, his stomach, his chest, had the warmth of Molly's body, seated on his shoulders and silent as though she didn't want to distract him from his sweet obsession.

Bérubé forced himself to think of a cow, an airplane, the wreck of a big ship, the *Satanic*, that he had heard stories about, of Hitler's moustache, of the toilets he had cleaned and washed for months and months. In his head one image was supreme, one image that hid the rest of the universe behind it: Bérubé saw, as though for the first time, Molly standing up near the bed, naked, her breasts spilling out of her brassiere; then he thought of the pleasure he had had. Ah! his pleasure had been so intense he had wept like a child.

Bérubé, completely swallowed up, could not pull himself out of the snow or even move his foot. It was making him dizzy. He let Molly down, jumped on her, and caught her mouth between his lips, trying to bite it. Roughly, he caressed her breasts.

"Oh! " complained Molly, who was floudering about. After a fierce struggle she succeeded in freeing an arm, and gave him a slap in the face. "Nothing but animals, these French Canadians. I don't want my dress to get creased," she said, to excuse herself.

He did not reply. He had decided simply to abandon her there, in the snow. He got up. Free of the load on his shoulders he was less troubled by the snow. He went away. Molly did not call him. Anyway, he would not have answered if she had called. Something warm tickled him in the corner of his mouth. He put his finger to it. It was blood.

"*La bon Dieu de Vierge!* "

He picked up a handful of snow and stopped up his wound.

"Let her freeze there standing in the snow, *la Vierge*. I won't let any woman break my jaw; not a whore, not an Anglaise. Not an Anglaise. Let her freeze there, *la Vierge*."

Bérubé turned around to see his wish come true. Almost disappearing in the snow because of her white dress, Molly was waving her arms about to call her husband, but she was quiet. Bérubé after savouring his triumph for a moment, cried: "Go ahead and freeze to death."

Lower down, at the foot of the mountain, Molly

noticed a group of men carrying a long box on their shoulders. "That French Canadian has got blood on my dress."

Bérubé arrived in the village alone; that was when he learned about Corriveau's death.

★ ★ ★ ★ ★

The gossips were saying, "Now that Amélie's got two men in the house she must be satisfied."

Amélie had started to prepare a meal. She was alone in the house. Saucepans sang on the wood fire, perfuming the kitchen. She wanted a man. Arthur had gone out; Henri was in the attic. She smiled. In a long caress she slid her hands over her bosom and slowly onto her belly and thighs. She stood up again, went to the stove, lifted the covers off the pots, the aroma of the roasting meat drifting out.

She tested it with her fork, checking to see how much longer the meat had to cook, replaced the cover and climbed upstairs. Amélie needed a man.

Was it Henri's turn, or Arthur's? Who had slept with her the last time. Her two men made her keep a strict accounting; that was very difficult.

Amélie wanted a man, and in a few minutes the meat would be burning on the roaring fire. She took the broom and, according to the code, rapped on the ceiling. Someone moved in the attic. The heavy trunks were pulled aside and the trap door opened.

"What is it?" asked Henri in a voice choked with sleep.

"Get down here, I need you."

"What for?"

"Hurry up, I can't wait till Arthur gets back."

"What for?" Henri repeated, hardly convinced.

"Get undressed and come here!"

"It's not my turn," he yawned. "I don't want to cut in when Arthur's away."

Amélie had already undone the buttons on her dress. Henri leapt from the attic. He started to undo his trousers.

"Hurry up," Amélie ordered, hurrying towards the bed. "I've got some meat on the stove."

"Hurry up," repeated Henri, "that's easy for you to say; a man isn't always ready."

He finished undressing, getting out of his clothes as though they were a thornbush.

"What's the weather like today?" he asked Amélie, who was already stretched out on the bed.

"Winter, same as yesterday."

"I know that. I know perfectly well that it's winter. I'm dying of cold up there in the attic."

"It's your own fault. If you'd been willing to go to war you wouldn't have to hide in an attic and be cold. Hurry up; thaw out."

"There isn't even a goddamn window in my attic. And the cracks in the ceiling are blocked up with ice. That's how I know it's winter."

"Hurry up. You can keep your wool socks on . . . Don't complain about nothing. If you weren't so well off in your attic you'd go to war. Come on."

Then Amélie became gentle. "And besides," she said with a smile, "you're not always in the attic . . ." Her

36

voice was caressing. "Isn't that right, Henri? "

Henri was undressed now. Rather bored by this tenderness and curious to see the village, he went to the window and pulled aside the curtain. The glass was covered with frost. He brought his mouth close to it and breathed out a long breath. Under the warmth of his breath the frost melted a little. Then Henri scratched with his fingernail.

"Henri! " begged Amélie, impatient.

He continued to scratch the frost until he could see. He stuck his eye into the little hole. Who was coming up the road?

"Amélie, there's something in the road."

"If you don't come here Henri, I'll get mad." Amélie, in her bed, was worked up. Henri continued to scratch at the frost. "Come see what I see, Amélie." "Henri, if you don't come and get on top of me right now it'll be a long time before you put your behind in my sheets."

"Come here, I tell you."

Persuaded by his insistence, Amélie got up and went to the window. Henri gave her his observation post. She looked for a long time, then drew back. Henri looked again.

A soldier was holding a bugle at the end of his arm, which was stretched out horizontally. A coffin followed behind him, carried by six other soldiers and enveloped in a flag. A woman in a white wedding gown was escorting the coffin. The cortège ended with the boys of the village who were marching solemnly along with it, their hockey sticks on their shoulders.

They passed in front of Amélie's house and disappeared towards the other end of the village.

"It's Corriveau," said Henri.

"Yes, it's Corriveau coming home."

Amélie returned to lie down on her bed. Her husband accompanied her.

Their embrace became more and more violent, and, for a moment, without their daring to admit it, they loved one another.

★ ★ ★ ★ ★

The door was narrow. It wasn't easy to bring the coffin into the house. The soldiers were very embarrassed not to be able to keep the symmetry of their movements. The door of the Corriveaus' little house had not been built to accommodate a coffin. The bearers put it down in the snow, calculated at what angle it could pass, studied how they should arrange themselves around it, argued. Finally the sergeant gave an order; they picked up the heavy coffin again, inclined it, placed it almost on edge, made themselves as narrow as possible, and finally succeeded in entering, out of breath and exhausted.

"Leave it now," grumbled old man Corriveau. "It's enough that he's dead, you don't have to swing him around like that."

The door opened into the kitchen. In the middle was a big wooden table.

"Put him there," said Mother Corriveau, "on the table. And put his head here, at this end. It's his place. Like that he'll feel more at home."

The English soldiers didn't understand the language

the old people were speaking. They knew it was French, but they had rarely heard it.

"On the table! " repeated Mr. Corriveau.

The carriers put the coffin back on their shoulders and looked around for a place to put it.

"On the table! " ordered Mother Corriveau.

The Anglais shrugged their shoulders to show that they did not understand. Mr. Corriveau was getting angry. He said, very loud, "On the table! We want him on the table! "

The sergeant smiled. He had understood. He gave a command. The obedient soliders turned towards the door: they were going to take the coffin outside.

Mr. Corriveau ran to the door and spread his arms to block their passage. "*Vieux pape de Christ*! They come and take him by force, they get him killed without asking our permission, and now we're going to have to use our fists to get him back from them." The old man, red with anger, threatened the sergeant with his fist; the latter wondered why everyone didn't speak English like he did.

"*Vieux pape de Christ*! "

"Put it on the table," said Molly in English. She had come in after carefully shaking the snow from her dress.

"What's she come here for, that one? " asked Mother Corriveau. "He's our dead."

When she saw the soldiers obey Molly, Mother Corriveau accepted her presence, and asked her, with an air of recognition on her face, "Tell them to take away the cover; our little boy is going to be too hot in there."

Molly translated. The soldiers gave Mother Corriveau a withering look. How dare she refer to the British flag as a "cover"! The old lady had no idea she had offended England; she would have been astounded if someone had told her that this "cover" was the flag her son had died for. If she had been told that, she would have kissed the flag as she kissed the relics of the tunic of the twenty-three-year-old Jesus Christ every night.

The sergeant decided to ignore the insult. The soldiers folded the flag, the sergeant blew on his bugle a plaint that made the windowpanes shudder and the villagers, already assembled around Corriveau, weep. The sound of the bugle stunned Anthyme Corriveau, who nervously dropped his pipe. He cursed his rotten teeth that couldn't hold a pipe any more. At twenty, Anthyme had had hard teeth that could crumble a glass, chew it. Now his rotten teeth were a sign that all his bones were going rotten too. He was so old, Anthyme, his sons were beginning to die. "When your sons begin to leave you, it won't be long before you go to join them."

"Anthyme," said his wife, "go find your screwdriver. I want to see if our boy's face has been all mashed up or if he knew enough to protect it like I told him. In all my letters I used to tell him, 'My child, think first of all of your face. A one-legged man, or even a man with no legs at all, is less frightening for a woman than a man with only one eye or no nose.' When he wrote back the dear child always said, 'I'm taking good care to protect my face.' Anthyme! I asked you for your screwdriver. I want that coffin opened."

Molly, in practising her trade, had learned several words of French. The French Canadians in Newfoundland liked Molly a lot. She explained, according to what she had understood, the Corriveaus' wish. The sergeant said, "No! No! No! No! "

His men shook their heads to say "No" too. Mother Corriveau took the sergeant's hand and squeezed it with all her might: she would have liked to squash it like an egg. The sergeant, with a courteous strength, freed himself. His face was pale, but he smiled.

The sergeant felt sorry for these ignorant French Canadians who did not even recognize their country's flag.

"Anthyme Corriveau, you're going to take your shotgun and get these *maudits* Anglais out of my house. They take my son from me, they let him get killed for me, and now they won't let me see him. Anthyme Corriveau, take out your shotgun and shoot them right between the buttocks, if they've got any."

Crushed by the heaviest despair, old man Corriveau relit his pipe. At this moment there was nothing more important than managing to light his pipe.

"Anthyme! " shouted his wife. "If you don't want to use your shotgun, give them a kick. And get busy! After that you're going to look for your screwdriver."

"*Vieille pipe de Christ*! You can ask me for my screwdriver as often as you want. I can't remember where I put it last time I . . . "

"Anthyme! Get these *maudits* Anglais out of this house! "

The old man put out his match; the flame was burning his fingers. He spoke after several puffs. "Mother, we can't do a thing. Whether you see him or not, our boy is gone."

Mother Corriveau said simply, "We're going to pray."

Her husband had reminded her of the most obvious fact: "We can't do anything," Anthyme had said. An entire life-time had taught them that they could do nothing. Mother Corriveau was no longer angry. It was with a gentle voice that she had said, "We're going to pray."

41

She knelt, her husband did the same, then the villagers who had come, then Molly, taking care not to crease her wedding dress. The old woman started the prayer, the prayer she had learned from the lips of her mother, who had learned it from hers: "Our Lady of the faithful dead: may he rest in peace among the saints of the Lord."

The seven soldiers knelt: the old lady was so astonished that she could not remember the rest of the formula.

"Anthyme," she muttered, "instead of getting all distracted while your son is burning in the fires of purgatory it might be a good thing if you'd pray for him. Your prayers will shorten his suffering. But then when I think of how you brought him up, I don't know if he's in purgatory or already in hell. Maybe he's in hell. In hell . . ."

She was choked by sobs. Anthyme started again, with the words of a man who has had to pray every time his wife threatens him with hell: "*Que le Seigneur des fidèles défont les lunes en paix dans la lumière du paradis.*"

Everyone replied, "Amen."

"*Je vous salue Marie, pleine et grasse, le Seigneur avez-vous et Bénedict et toutes les femmes et le fruit de vos entailles, Albanie.*"

"Amen."

The incantation was taken up several times. Then, Anthyme Corriveau was praying alone. No one was replying to his invocations any more. What was going on? He continued to pray, but he opened his eyes. Everyone was looking at his wife, who was lost in a happy dream. She was smiling.

The Blessed Virgin had given her mother's heart to

42

understand that her son was in heaven. All of his sins, his oaths, his blasphemies, the caresses he had given the girls of the village, and especially the girls in the old country where had had gone to war, his drunken evenings when he used to go walking in the village throwing his clothes in the snow, the evenings when bare-chested and drunk her son would raise his fist to Heaven and shout, "God, the proof that you don't exist is that you aren't striking me down right now," all these sins of Corriveau had been pardoned; the Blessed Virgin had breathed it to his mother.

If the hand of God had not struck down Corriveau on those nights it had weighed on the roofs of the houses. People in the village would not forget those alcoholic evenings, even if God had forgiven Corriveau for them. His mother felt in her soul the peace that must now be her child's. Her son had been pardoned because he had died in the war. The old lady felt in her heart that God was obliged to pardon soldiers who had died in the war.

Her son had been reclothed in the immaculate gown of the elect. He was beautiful. He had changed a little since he had gone off to war. A mother gets used to seeing her children look more and more like strangers. Dying transforms a face too. Mother Corriveau saw her son among the angels. She would have liked him to lower his eyes towards her, but he was completely absorbed in the prayer that he was murmuring, smiling. The old lady wept, but she wept for joy. She rose.

"Take my son out of the kitchen and put him in the living room. We're going to eat. I've made twenty-one *tourtières*. Anthyme, go dig up five or six bottles of cider."

★ ★ ★ ★ ★

43

Furniture was shifted to free a wall against which the coffin was placed. In front of it rows of chairs were arranged, like in church. Anthyme had gone to the shed to look for some big cherry-wood stumps that would make solid legs for the coffin. Mother Corriveau had taken all her candles from the drawers, the tallow ones and those made of beeswax, the ones that had been blessed and the others. The blessed ones had protected her family during thunder and lightning; the others served very well for giving light when the electricity was cut off by storms or by ice on the wires. The soldiers stood at attention. Anthyme, with some other villagers, installed himself in front of them and fell asleep immediately, as he always did when he sat down. Mother Corriveau stuffed her stove with wood, because twenty-one *tourtières* would not be enough. "When there's a dead person in the house the living have to eat for those who have passed away."

"Everyone" as Anthyme said — even the villagers who had not spoken to the Corriveaus for ten years — had arrived or were on their way, all dressed in black.

"We're going to say a little prayer so that his soul will requiescat in pace."

On her knees, hands joined on the coffin, Molly prayed. What prayer could she say, she who could speak only English? "She must pray to her God, the English God," thought Anthyme. "The God of the English and the God of the French Canadians couldn't be the same one; that isn't possible. The English protestants are damned, so there couldn't be a God for the damned in hell. She isn't praying at all; she's only pretending."

Mother Corriveau interrupted her work for a minute to look at Molly. "I didn't think of asking her, but she could be the wife of our son . . . Maybe our little boy got married during a break when there wasn't any war. Maybe he told us about his marriage in a letter that was bombed by the Germans. There's no way of knowing. This war is turning life inside out. Anyway, if she is our son's wife we'll keep her with us just like our own daugher . . . I'll talk to her about that later. It's not a question you can easily ask a young girl who has just been married when there's a dead man in the house and the dead man has married her just a couple of days before."

To keep awake Anthyme got up and was leaning against the doorframe. He was contemplating Molly's lush body: her breasts — it would have taken both Anthyme's hands to hold just one — where they swelled out her bodice, and her waist, which heralded buttocks that could make a man lose his head. Looking at Molly made him young, gave him a rest from Mother Corriveau all swallowed up in her own fat.

Suddenly the door was opened, almost torn off its hinges, by a kick that shook the whole house. Everyone found themselves, prayers on their lips, in the kitchen. A soldier was standing on the doorstep, paralysed before all those people whom he recognized, pale and frightened. It was Bérubé.

"I've come to get my wife," he explained. "They said Molly was here with the *maudits* Anglais." He spoke almost politely.

"She's in there," indicated Mother Corriveau, relieved now that Molly was not the wife of her son. "Don't put your dirty feet on the rug. And before you enter a house, you ask permission."

"I'm sorry."

"Don't say that, you cheeky little hoodlum. When

you were little you used to say 'excuse me.' It always meant you were going to come back and do something worse."

Molly understood, but she didn't turn around. She stayed alone on her knees with Corriveau. Bérubé ran into the living room, grabbed Molly by the arm, shook her, and with his other hand he slapped her.

"Whore! "

Molly didn't try to protect herself.

"When you're married you don't turn on the charm, either to dead men or living ones."

Molly's nose was bleeding. Her dress would be stained.

"I'm going to make you understand you're my wife and not a whore."

He struck her with both hands. Molly collapsed, wedged between the foot of the coffin and the wall. Bérubé brought back his big leather boot and prepared to kick.

"Atten — shun! ! ! " thundered the guttural voice of the sergeant.

Bérubé stood at attention. He clicked his heels. Bérubé was nothing but a ball of obedient muscles. The sergeant who had barked out the order walked towards Bérubé and gave him a steely look. Bérubé waited to be hit. The sergeant, two steps away from him, breathed in his face. Bérubé felt as if his eyes were melting and trickling down his cheeks; in fact, he was crying. He was crying because there was nothing he could do. Bérubé felt like attacking the sergeant, dislocating his jaw, blackening his eyes, making him bleed.

After a long, silent confrontation the sergeant said, "Dismiss."

Bérubé turned on his heel and Molly followed him, holding his arm. Mother Corriveau detained them just as they were going out. "As far as I'm concerned I don't want you not to stay. I don't want you to have to go out in the snow. Even dogs don't go out at this hour. I offer you my boy's room; he doesn't need to sleep now."

In the bedroom Molly took off her dress.

"Whore of a woman," said Bérubé as he took down his pants. He was laughing. Undressed, he lay down against her; they embraced, the world spun around them. For a moment they were happy.

Bérubé opened his eyes abruptly and said, "Corriveau isn't going to like this, us having fun, making love in his bed."

★ ★ ★ ★ ★

Night darkened the snow. The candle flames were dancing on the flag-covered coffin. The living-room was filled with men and women from the village packed tightly against one another. The soldiers were lined up against the wall, motionless, erect, looking towards Corriveau, silent. Everyone was praying, mumbling "Mother of God," "Save us sinners," "At the hour of our death": tirelessly they repeated the phrases, "Forgive us our mortal faults," "Welcome them into the kingdom of the Father," "Re-quiescat-in-pace"; they purred "God," "Amen," "Holy

47

Ghost," "Deliver him from the claws of the devil." Pronouncing these prayers they began to miss Corriveau; they were sorry that they had not liked him when he was among them, before the war; they prayed loudly as though Corriveau could hear them and recognize their voices, as if their prayers could make Corriveau happy under his British flag. The villagers were alive, they were praying to remind themselves, to remember that they were not with Corriveau, that their life was not over; and all the time thinking they were praying for Corriveau's salvation, it was their own joy in being alive that they proclaimed in their sad prayers. The happier they were the more they prayed, and the little flames on Corriveau's coffin wavered, danced, as though they were trying to free themselves from their wicks. Shadow and light played on the wall, making strange designs that perhaps meant something. The air disturbed the flag a little. It seemed as if Corriveau was going to get up. They prayed, they murmured, they whispered; they finished their prayers, began again; they swallowed their words to pray more quickly, while in the kitchen Mother Corriveau beat at her pie dough with her fists, and the sweat ran down her back, onto her forehead, into her eyes; she wiped it with her floury hands. Her face was white with flour and the sweat ran into the flour. She stopped a drop that was tickling between her breasts, and started again to prepare her pastry, stirring, rolling, twisting, while on the stove the pork was crackling in its boiling fat.

"Don't go to too much trouble, Mother Corriveau."

"When there's a dead man in the house the house shouldn't smell of death."

She opened the oven. The golden crust whispered at its contact with the air and a perfume that reawakened appetites spread through the kitchen. One by one the villagers got up, abandoned their prayers and Corriveau, and went into the kitchen. Mother Corriveau welcomed them with a plate on which she had put a quarter of a *tourtière* under a sauce made of a mixture of apples, strawberries, bilberries and currants. As for Anthyme, he was holding out a glass filled with foaming cider. For years he had been making his cider in the fall when, as he said, "The wind is ready to scratch the apples." Then he buried his bottles in the cellar where they remained hidden in the ground for a very long time. His children became men and the bottles were still in the ground. At times, on great occasions, Anthyme would parsimoniously draw out a bottle and quickly fill in the hole so that, as he said, "The light of the cider won't get out." Over the years Anthyme's cider became charged with marvellous forces in the earth.

A bottle in each hand, Anthyme was now looking for empty glasses. When a glass was filled the old man wore a smile like God the creator.

Meanwhile, in the living room, the tide of prayers subsided; people were talking, laughing, arguing; in the kitchen they ate and drank and were happy, while Mother Corriveau looked on with brimming eyes. From time to time she wiped a tear that came as she thought of her son, loved by so many people: not only the people from the village, but also the army, which had sent a delegation of seven soldiers because her son had given his life in the war. So many people joined together for her son; Mother Corriveau could have no finer consolation. She wouldn't have believed that her son was so well-liked.

They ate and prayed; they were thirsty and hungry; they prayed again, they smoked and drank. They had the whole night before them.

"You're not trying to tell me there are really men like that in town!"

"You mean if our boys leave home to work in town they'll turn into homosexuals?"

The third blew his nose too energetically; his eyes were filled with tears. "Hey, have you forgotten there's a war on? Our boys don't have to go off to town any more."

The first kept to his story. "I'm telling you, I'm not lying."

Father Anthyme arrived with his bottle of cider and filled their glasses.

"I mean it," the first one went on, "I've seen two . . ."

"Two what?"

"Two homosexuals. When I went to town. Two homosexuals pushing a baby carriage."

The three men laughed until they couldn't stand up. They choked and chortled, they wept, they laughed till they seemed about to burst. Their faces were red. When they stopped laughing, the first man took up his story again.

"Two homosexuals. When I noticed their baby carriage I went up to them. I couldn't believe they were taking a baby for a walk. I looked in the carriage and there inside it was a little homosexual!"

The other two were genuinely astonished. "Things are happening nowadays you wouldn't have thought possible thirty years ago."

"You don't even know any more if there's a God. There are people who say if there was a God he wouldn't be allowing this war."

"But there have always been wars, or it seems like it."

"Then that means maybe there's no God."

"You could talk about something else," suggested Louisiana, who had heard them even though she had been gossiping in another group. "That takes some nerve, saying there's no God when a little boy from the village is roasting in purgatory."

The wife of the man who had told the anecdote had heard too. "If you go on blaspheming I'm taking you home to bed, and your hands will stay on top of the covers."

At least twelve men had a good laugh at her threat.

The man who had been caught out indicated the living room with his nose, and pointed his finger towards Corriveau. "Fatso, if it was your son in there, would you still believe there was a God?"

"I'd believe it because He is everywhere, even in the heads of idiots like you."

"According to you, God would be in your big tits." Anthyme came to serve him some cider. The man drank his glassful in one gulp.

"I didn't say there isn't a God, and I didn't say there is one. Me, I don't know. If Corriveau has seen him, let him raise his hand. Me, I don't know."

Father Corriveau, who was listening, stupefied, with his two bottles of cider, had nothing to say. He refilled the glass.

"It's not my child who's in the coffin," the man said; "it's yours, Anthyme."

"So it is; you shouldn't have that trouble," said Anthyme to the weeping man; "It's my boy, not yours."

"It's not my boy in the coffin, but I wonder: if there is a God, why does he spend so much time sending

51

children into these holes? Why, Anthyme? "

"An old man in a coffin, I find that just as hard to look at as a young one." Anthyme was weeping too.

The villagers were very gay. "Ha! Ha! " laughed one of them. "I've seen some nice behinds, some real nice ones. (Not my wife's, of course.) So I say to myself, if there are nice behinds like that on earth, what is there going to be in Heaven? "

"What a lot of hell Corriveau'll raise! When he was alive he was quite a rooster."

"Father Anthyme, we haven't got any cider! "

Mother Corriveau took more *tourtières* from the oven. The whole house was an oven that smelled of fat golden pork. Through this perfume floated phrases from prayers: *"Salut pleine et grasse"*; *"Entrailles ébenies"*; *"Pour nous pauvres pêcheurs"*; *"Repas éternel"*; these mingled with pungent clouds of tobacco smoke. They had to stay all night. The soldiers remained at attention, against their wall. There were distractions for the young girls as they prayed: they forgot the words of their Ave's as they admired how handsome the soldiers were, these Anglais who didn't have coarse, dark hairs on their cheeks but beautiful fair skin; it would be good to put their lips there.

It wasn't human for them to stay fixed there all night, stiff and motionless. It's not a position for the living. The Corriveaus went to offer them cider or *tourtière*, but the soldiers refused anything.

"Why don't you drink a little glass of cider? " asked Anthyme.

"Have a little piece of my *tourtière* then," coaxed his wife.

The Anglais didn't budge, didn't even answer "No" at the ends of their lips.

52

"They turn up their noses at our food," thought Anthyme.

Mother Corriveau found the laughter too generous. "You're going to wake up my son."

"Would you like a little glass of cider? " offered Anthyme, filling the glass before he had an answer.

In the living room, they were praying: "Jesus Christ," "So be it," "Save us," "The eternal flames"; they were juggling syllables, words, as they prayed, rushing through their prayers. The faster they prayed the sooner Corriveau would leave the flames of purgatory. And if he was condemned to the eternal fires of hell perhaps their prayers would ease the burning.

In the kitchen the people were talking:

"I'd bet my dog that if you climb on a woman three times a day, not counting the nights, that's hard on the heart."

"It's better to kill yourself by climbing on your wife than by working."

"Pig! "

The one who had made the accusation was a bachelor. The other reproached him. "I like people who climb on their wives better than the ones who enjoy themselves all alone like bachelors."

The bachelor was used to this. "I prefer climbing on other men's wives."

The villagers roared with laughter, they belched, they swallowed mouthfuls of cider, and without retying their ties they went, by common consent, into the living room to pray. Those who were in the living room got up and went into the kitchen, where Mother Corriveau never stopped caressing her *tourtières*, and Anthyme worked just as hard filling glasses with cider.

53

"Listen, here's a good one."

"I'm not in the habit of listening in on dirty stories," insisted Anthyme, who wanted to hear the story. "But tonight, laughing a little might help me forget my sad sorrow. Losing my boy has made me suffer as much as if both my arms had been torn off. Worse, even. I can still see myself, one morning in spring. He had come home well after sunrise. His shirt was undone. It was stained with blood. A white shirt. His lip was as thick as my fist. His left eye, or maybe it was the right, was closed it was so swollen. I stood in the doorway of his bedroom and I said, 'We won't argue. Just go back where you came from and don't set foot in this house again, drunkard.' He left, and he's come back to us today."

Anthyme could not talk any more. He was sobbing. His wife was looking at him hard, like someone who will not allow herself to be tender.

"He's drunk too much, the dirty old man. He throws his sons out the door, but he doesn't notice that it's him they take after. He gives everybody cider but he doesn't forget himself. He takes advantage of the death of his son to let himself get drunk like an animal. You old bum, you're drunk."

"I'm sad, wife, I've never been so sad."

"Come on Anthyme, give me a little cider and don't cry. What the good Lord has taken away he'll give you back a hundredfold."

"At my age, you know I can't make another boy. Not with my wife, anyway . . . "

"Drink a little faster, Father Anthyme, and listen to my story."

"My wife doesn't want me to drink."

"You're too sad. It's bad luck to be as sad as you are.

You need a little distraction. Listen to this; it's a good one . . . Once there was . . ."

The raconteur put his arm around Anthyme's shoulders and told him, in a tone confidential enough to attract the curious: "Once a young girl from town came to my place, a cousin of mine. She asked if she could milk a cow. Sit on my little stool, I told her; you know what to do? — Yes. I went on to something else. I came back five minutes later. She was still sitting beside the cow, tickling the tits with the ends of her fingers, caressing them tenderly. Would you mind telling me what you're doing there? I asked her. — I'm making them hard, Uncle."

They laughed heartily till they choked; they struck their thighs and punched one another. They had never heard such a funny story. Anthyme had tears in his eyes, and laugh! right now he was laughing so hard, shaking so much, that he was spilling cider on the floor.

"You're going to kill me," he said.

And he went on to another group where the thirst was great. In the living room, on Corriveau's coffin, the candleflame was clinging stubbornly.

Anthyme Corriveau found himself again, after he had served the drinks, in front of the storyteller, who was proud of his success and still enjoying it.

"Father Anthyme, that story was told to me by your son. He should be laughing at it with us."

"Oh! " said Anthyme, "he shouldn't want to laugh."

★ ★ ★ ★ ★

Mother Corriveau was still cooking her *tourtières*. She was soaked in sweat as though she had been caught in a storm. She was tearing around the stove. Feeling something sticking into her breast she stuck her hand into her bodice. She had forgotten, in her grief, the letter the sergeant had presented to her when he arrived.

"Anthyme," she ordered, drawing the letter out from between her breasts, "come here. I forgot."

She waved the letter.

"Come here. I've got a letter from my boy."

"From our boy," Anthyme corrected. "Open it. Hurry up."

Because of this letter Corriveau was alive. They forgot that their child was lying in his coffin. The old lady feverishly tore open the envelope. It wasn't true that he was dead; he had written. The letter would correct the facts. The villagers spread the word from one group to the next that the Corriveaus had received a letter from their son. They continued to laugh, to eat, to drink, to pray. Mother Corriveau started slowly to puzzle out the letter that had been found in her son's pocket.

"My dearest parents,

I won't write you very much because I have to keep my steel helmet on my head and if I think too hard the heat could melt my helmet and then it wouldn't protect me very well. The socks mother sent me are really warm. Give me news about my brothers. Have any of them got themselves killed? As for my sisters, they're probably still washing their dishes and diapers. I'd rather get a shell in the rear than think about all that. I've won a decoration; it's nice. The more decorations you have, the farther you stay from the Germans." (Everyone insisted, so Mother Corriveau started reading this part again.) "I've won a decoration . . . "

56

Father Corriveau, amazed, snatched the letter from his wife and proclaimed, pushing people around in his excitement, "My boy got a decoration! My boy won a decoration! "

From all their hearts, from the bottoms of the hearts of those who were praying and those who were drinking, a hymn was raised up that made the ceiling shake:

Il a gagné ses épaulettes
Maluron malurette
Il a gagné ses épaulettes
Maluron maluré.

★ ★ ★ ★ ★

Eventually the feast spread to the living room too. The flag covering Corriveau's coffin became a tablecloth where plates and glasses were left and cider was spilled. People sitting at the kitchen table leaned against a wall because it was hard to keep your balance with a plate in one hand, a glass of cider in the other, fat from the *tourtière* streaming down cheeks and chin; or they kept their heads high and dry on a pile of greasy dishes, or else standing in the doorway which was open to the snow and cold, they tried to vomit to get rid of their dizziness; or they put both hands on Antoinette's generous backside or tried to see through the wool covering Philomène's breasts; and they ate juicy *tourtière* in the living room, in the odour of the candles which were going out, and they prayed in the heavy odour of the kitchen where the smell of grease mingled with that of the sweat of the men and women.

They prayed: *"Sainte-Marie pleine et grasse, le seigneur, avez-vous? Entrez toutes les femmes . . . "*

These people did not doubt that their prayer would be understood. They prayed with all their strength as men, all their strength as women who had borne children. They did not ask God for Corriveau to come back on earth; they begged God quite simply not to abandon him for too long in the flames of purgatory. Corriveau couldn't be in hell. He was a boy from the village, and it would have seemed unfair to these villagers for one of their children to be condemned to the eternal flames. Perhaps some people deserved a very long time in purgatory, but no one really deserved hell.

Amélie had come with Arthur while Henri, her deserter husband, remained cowering in his attic, well protected by the heavy trunks slid across the trapdoor.

"In purgatory the fire doesn't hurt as much as in hell. You know that you can get out of purgatory; you think of that while you're burning. Then the fire doesn't bite so bad. So let us pray for the fire of purgatory to purify Corriveau. Hail Mary . . . "

Amélie strung all her prayers end to end, formulas learned at school, responses from her little catechism, and she felt that she was right.

"Let us pray again," she said.

How could a woman leading a dishonest life with two men in her house be so pious? How could she explain supernatural things about religion and hell with so much wisdom? Despite her impure life Amélie was a good woman. Occasions like this evening were fortunate, people would say: you have to have deaths and burials from time to time to remember the goodness of people. The villagers felt a great warmth in their hearts: it wasn't possible that there was a hell. To imaginations steeped in pork fat and cider, the flames of hell were scarcely bigger than the candleflames on Corriveau's coffin. The flames could not burn through all eternity; all the fires they were familiar with were extinguished after a certain time: fires made to clear the land, or wood fires, or the fires of love. An eternal flame seemed impossible. Only God is eternal, and as Corriveau was a boy from the village where people are good despite their weaknesses, he would not stay long in purgatory. They would bring him out through the strength of their prayers: perhaps he was out even now.

"*Memento domine domini domino . . .*"

"*Requiescat in pace!* "

Mother Corriveau was still filling the plates held out to her like starving mouths; in the cellar Anthyme was unearthing new bottles of cider.

The Anglais were at attention, impassive, like statues. Even their eyes did not move. Nobody noticed them. They were part of the décor, like the windows, the lamps, the crucifix, the coffin, the furniture. If someone had observed them up close he would have noticed a gesture of disdain at the edges of their nostrils and the creases of their lips.

"What a bunch of savages, these French Canadians! "

They neither moved nor looked at one another. They were made of wood. They didn't even sweat.

Hands in their pockets, Jos and Pit, the latter leaning against the coffin, were chatting. "That damn Corriveau, I'd like to know what he's thinking about in his coffin with all these women prowling around him."

"There are lots of women going to cry when he's buried."

"Some of them are going to be dreaming about a ghost with soft hands."

"Me, I'll stick my hand in shit if he hasn't undressed at least twenty-two of the women here: Amélie, Rosalia, Alma, Théodelia, Joséphine, Arthurise, Zélia . . ."

"So where does that get him? " Jos cut in: "Now Corriveau's lying between his four boards all by himself. He won't get up again."

"Albina," Pit continued, "Léopoldine, Patricia, then your wife . . ."

"What are you talking about, *Calvaire*? "

"I'm telling the truth."

Before he had pronounced the last syllable Pit received a fist in his teeth. He fell over backwards among the plates and glasses, onto Corriveau's coffin. The soldiers moved forward in unison, took hold of the two men, threw them out the open door into the snow, and returned to take up their post again.

The two enemies could be heard shouting and swearing in the cold air. While they tore at each other, the rest were praying for Corriveau's salvation.

"Grant him eternal salvation. Forgive him his trespasses."

They stopped eating. They did not dare to raise another glass to their lips. Everyone was praying. The winter became silent once more.

"They've killed each other," moaned one of the women.

Then the two men appeared in the doorway, faces bloody and blue, snowy, their clothes torn, arms around each other.

"It's not worth going to the bother of fighting if Corriveau isn't in it," Pit explained.

They moved towards the coffin. "You missed a *Vierge* of a good fight," Jos said.

Pit put two fingers into his mouth. He was missing some teeth.

"Peace deserves a glass of cider! " proclaimed Anthyme.

★ ★ ★ ★ ★

Molly was watching Bérubé sleep, his head on his folded tunic which served as a pillow. She had awakened because she was cold. She pressed against his chest. The warmth of this sleeping man felt good. Bérubé was snoring. Each time he exhaled he enveloped Molly in a cloud that smelled of Scotch and rotten sausage.

"What a stink — a sleeping man! "

She turned her head to avoid the disagreeable odour, but she remained fastened to him, flesh against flesh. She slid her arm under Bérubé's shoulder and pressed her chest a little more closely against his, as though she wanted to merge her breasts with his hard torso. Bérubé's sex slowly rose. Near him, overcome by a burning dizziness, Molly would have liked to throw herself into him, as into a bottomless pit. Downstairs people were laughing, praying too, and under his flag Corriveau was dead. He would never laugh again, never pray again, never eat or see the snow or a woman or make love. With her whole mouth Molly kissed the sleeper; she would have liked to take his breath away. Bérubé stirred a little, and Molly felt his flesh come alive, rouse itself from sleep.

She sighed, "Darling, let's make love. I'm afraid you'll die too."

Bérubé moved, grunted, farted.

"Let's make love, please."

Bérubé rolled onto Molly. It was death that they stabbed at, violently.

★ ★ ★ ★ ★

Three sudden little knocks at the living-room window above Corriveau's coffin made everyone shudder. The villagers were quiet, listening. Every time someone dies, inexplicable things happen. The soul of the dead person does not want to leave the earth. Now nothing disturbed the silence. The villagers pricked up their ears: all they could hear was their own breathing, hoarse from fear. The cold twisted the beams in the whining walls. The silence was sharp enough to cut a throat.

Three little blows shook the window again. The villagers looked at each other questioningly. They were not mistaken; they had certainly heard it. The men stuck their hands in their pockets, stiffening their chests in a challenging way. The women pressed against the men. Less terrified than the others, Anthyme said, "Something's going on at the window."

He pulled the curtain, which was never opened. Night had fallen long ago. It was very black outside the window. The eyes of the villagers were fixed on the blackness.

62

"If there was a noise at the window it's because somebody's out there," reasoned Mother Corriveau. "Have a better look, Anthyme, and not with your eyes shut."

"Maybe it isn't something you can see," suggested one of the women.

Then a shadow moved in the shadows. Anthyme took a candle from the coffin and approached the window. The light shone first of all on the sparkling frost. In the centre of the frame the glass was bare, but Anthyme could see nothing but his reflection.

The knocking began again.

"*Vieille pipe de Christ,*" he swore. "If you want to come in, come in the door."

A little voice from the other side of the window tried to make itself stronger than the wind. "Don't you recognize me?" she asked.

"*Vieille pipe de Christ*, if you'd let us see you maybe I'd recognize you. Are you ashamed of your face?"

"Open up!" the little voice implored. "It's me."

"*Vieux pape de Christ*, don't you know the difference between a door and a window?"

Anthyme climbed up with both feet on his son's coffin.

"Open . . ."

"Open!" repeated Anthyme. "*Baptême*! It isn't summer!"

"It's me, Esmalda!"

"Esmalda! *Vieille pipe du petit Jésus*! Esmalda! It's my daughter Esmalda, the nun," Anthyme explained. "It's our little nun. Come in, little Memalda!"

"The blessed rule of our community forbids me to enter my father's house."

"Little Esmalda!" Mother Corriveau cried with delight. "My little Esmalda! I haven't seen her since the morning when she left with her little suitcase that had nothing in it but her rosary; she left me a lock of her hair, beautiful blonde hair and I hung it at the feet of Christ on the crucifix." She was weeping with joy; she rubbed her eyes to wipe the tears. "My little Esmalda! Our little saint! "

The villagers got on their knees and bowed their heads.

"I'm not allowed to come into my father's house."

"*Vieille pipe de Christ*! I'd like to see anybody try and stop you from coming into your father's house."

". . . and your mother's. Come and get warm. And I've made some good *tourtières*. Don't stay outside."

"But I must obey."

"I'm your father. If you didn't have me the good sisters in your community wouldn't be able to forbid you to enter my house."

"I must obey."

"*Vieux pape* . . . "

His wife cut him off. "Anthyme, you don't understand a thing about holy matters! "

Esmalda's face near the window pane, her breath and her voice, her warmth, had enlarged a circle in the frost. You could make out her face more clearly, though it was still flooded in darkness.

"I would like to pray for my brother. Open the window."

"Come in by the door," shouted Anthyme. "We're glad to see you. The window will *not* be opened. It isn't summer. If you don't want to take the trouble to come in to see your little brother who was killed in the war you can stay outside and go back with the women who ask you to turn your nose up at the people who brought you into the world."

Mother Corriveau interrupted. "Anthyme, go and get the screwdriver and the hammer. Are you going to refuse hospitality to a little sister of Jesus? "

Using the screwdriver like a wedge, which he struck with the hammer into the space between the window and the frame, Anthyme tried to pull the window out of the ice. Although he hit it with the hammer and his shoulder, the window remained fixed in its place.

Arsène and Jos joined Anthyme on the coffin. The three of them pulled away the window the way you tear cloth.

A cold wind blew into the living room. The nun's face appeared, under her coif, rumpled in the lamplight. "It's good to come back to the house of one's parents, dead or alive," she declared.

Soaked in sweat, the villagers were shivering now. The sweat turned to ice on their backs.

The nun's head was motionless. A thin smile uncovered her sharp teeth.

"Who is dead? Who is alive? Perhaps the dead man is alive. Perhaps the living are dead."

The villagers crossed themselves.

"Sin may have killed the person who is alive. Who is without sin? Grace, the gift of God, may have revived someone who is dead. Who has the grace of God? " Then Esmalda was quiet. She looked at the villagers assembled before Corriveau's coffin. She looked a long time at each one, trying to recognize them. She had not seen them for many years, since her adolescence. She noted how voracious time had been, how it had ravaged the people of the village. When she recognized someone she smiled less

65

parsimoniously. They would not forget that smile.

"All together, men can damn a soul. All together, they cannot save a soul that has been damned. All together, men can lead one of their own behind the door that opens only once, and behind which eternity is a fire. But all together men cannot have one of their own admitted into the kingdom of the Father."

"Hail Mary," implored a voice which sounded like the last cry before the shipwreck.

The villagers replied in chorus. "The Lord is with you; have mercy on us poor sinners."

The nun waited for the end of the prayer; then she said, "I won't ask you to open the coffin to see my brother. If he has been damned I will not recognize his face; the face of one who has been damned is like a tortured demon. And if he has been saved I am not worthy of setting my eyes upon the face of an angel chosen by God."

"Hail Mary . . . " began another voice, as if it wanted to chase away what it had heard.

"Forgive us sinners! "

The nun lowered her head over her brother, gathered herself together for a moment, prayed in silence, and then raised her eyes to the villagers. "All men live together, but they follow different paths. But there is only one path, the one that leads to God."

The nun's decayed teeth could be seen in her rather sad smile. "How sweet it is to come back among one's own people! "

She turned around and disappeared into the night and the snow.

"She's a saint! " exclaimed Mother Corriveau.

"Let's shut that window fast," said Anthyme.

★ ★ ★ ★ ★

Stretching out his arms to show how long the pig was that he had killed for Anthyme, that was now being eaten chopped up in Mother Corriveau's *tourtières*, Arsène awkwardly bumped into the man next to him. The glass he was holding broke and slashed Arthur's cheek. Blood spurted out. Arthur stopped up the wound with the sleeve of his jacket. Amélie held him by the arm.

"Arthur, don't go and dirty my Sunday clothes. Blood stains don't come out."

Arthur refused to sit down. He remained standing in the middle of the kitchen. The villagers formed a circle around him to watch the blood flow. Arthur was amazed to see so much blood gushing out of such a little cut. He felt as if he was being drained of his contents like a bottle. When he started to bring his hand up to the wound, to put pressure on it and ease the flow of blood, Amélie lowered his arm. He was surprised that the blood was so red. Dazed, he put his hand on the wound again, and the blood burned his fingers, flowing onto his hand, his fist, his suit.

"What a baby!" said Amélie. "I tell him not to put his hands in his blood, but he can't resist it."

Anthyme arrived with a towel. He soaked it in cider. "Cider's good for the blood."

"Arthur's bleeding like the pig I killed."

"Instead of laughing," suggested Amélie, "how about bringing me some snow?"

Several men went out and came back with their hands full of snow. Amélie got busy and applied some to Arthur's wound. He grimaced because of the cold. The snow, all red from the blood, dropped onto the floor where it melted. Arsène, who was responsible for the

67

wound, could only apologize awkwardly.

"If I'd hit you a litte harder they'd be burying you with Corriveau."

Arsène laughed derisively. Everyone laughed. The clothing of Arthur and Amélie was red with blood. Grouped around them, everyone contemplated all the blood.

"Arthur didn't want to go to the war, but he looks as good as a lovely war wounded."

"Keep quiet," a woman begged.

"A handsome wounded man isn't as sad as a handsome man dead in the war," insisted Mother Corriveau who, after the accident, had returned to her pastry, in which a tear fell, and to her *tourtières* crackling in the oven.

Arsène insisted. "Seeing that much blood and a face chopped up so nice makes me sorry I didn't go to the war. Arthur makes me want to go to war. I think that having a German at your feet, losing all his goddamn German blood, that must satisfy a man. But it seems as if our soldiers don't see the Germans when they lose their blood. Our soldiers shoot their little rifles, then they go right away and hide, pissing in their pants for fear they've caught a German, because the Germans know how to defend themselves."

"Shut your big yaps! " shouted a demented voice that terrified the villagers. "Shut your yaps," the same voice repeated more calmly.

★ ★ ★ ★ ★

Bérubé appeared on the staircase, barechested, his face flat as though he had no eyes, barefoot, his khaki trousers too wide and his fly open.

"Shut up! "

No one opened his mouth. His cries had stifled their laughter and their prayers. The men, anticipating a good fight, didn't dare put down their glasses and plates. Rosaries were still in the hands of the women. Bérubé came down the last step buttoning himself up. They cleared a path for him, stepping back as he approached. He punched several stomachs, several breasts, and found himself in front of Arsène, who was convulsed. But his laughter was stopped in his throat when Bérubé grabbed him by the jacket. Buttons flew, cloth tore. The villagers were still as mice.

"*Calice de ciboire d'hostie! Christ en bicyclette sur son Calvaire!* So you think we enjoy ourselves in the war? You pile of shit! War is funny? I'll show you what the war's all about. You'll laugh."

While he was spitting his blasphemies Bérubé was hitting Arsène in the face ("*maudit ciboire de Christ!* "), not with his fist but with his open hand, and Arsène's big face was twisted with pain. Bérubé's eyes were red, and Arsène's big face was swinging with the blows ("*cochon de tabernacle!* "); his jacket was in shreds, his shirt was torn. Bérubé was in full cry.

"Oh! " cried Zeldina, "I've peed on the floor! "

"Shut up or I'll make you lick it up! "

He pushed Arsène against a wall, and tossed him about until the house shook.

"Ah! " he said, "soldiers have lots of fun in the war! War is fun! You don't know anything but the asses on your cows that look like your wives. It's funny, the war.

You like having Corriveau there in his coffin; he can't laugh any more, he'll never be able to laugh any more, *crucifix*! "

Bérubé could no longer shout or swear or speak. He was choked by his bitter anger; his eyes burned, and like a child he burst into sobs.

Was he the devil in flesh and blood? Terrified, the villagers stopped their prayers.

Arsène, waiting to take advantage of Bérubé's softening up to get away, took a chance and moved his foot. There was no reaction to his movement; Bérubé hadn't noticed it. Then Arsène threw himself forward. But Bérubé had caught up with him again. He held his head tight in the vise of his hands. "War is funny, eh, you big shit? I'll make a man out of you! Forward march! "

Bérubé pushed him, shoved him towards the mirror hanging on the kitchen wall. The villagers dispersed, closed their ears, broke glasses and plates, spilled cider on their coats and jackets. Bérubé flattened Arsène's face against the mirror.

"We have fun in the war, do we? It's a funny man who has a bloody face like a crushed strawberry. Laugh! There's nothing funnier than the war."

Arsène didn't dare move a pore of his skin.

"I told you to laugh," Bérubé repeated, punching his ears.

Arsène looked in the mirror and saw his rotten, tobacco-stained teeth; they were revealed as his lips unstuck and were clenched into a kind of smile.

"Laugh! "

Bérubé struck Arsène. The blows resounded and echoed in his head, which felt immense. His head felt as if it was going to burst, and his brains come out through his eyes.

"War's funny. Laugh."

Finally, Arsène succeeded in releasing a loud, phony laugh.

"So you laugh when men get themselves massacred by the goddamn Germans. I'll make you understand, by the sweet shit of holy Jesus."

Once more he struck, crushing his head between his two hands. After several blows Bérubé stopped the torture.

"Tell us what you see in the mirror."

"I see myself," Arsène replied fearfully.

"You see a big pile of shit. Have a good look. What do you see in the mirror? "

Bérubé grabbed Arsène by the neck and shook him until he begged for mercy. Then Bérubé calmed down. "In the war you have to look carefully; you have to see everything. Looking is learning. You learn everything through the seat of your pants. Watch out."

He let fly a few kicks.

"Okay," asked Bérubé, "what do you see if you look in the mirror? "

"I see Arsène."

"He doesn't understand a thing."

Bérubé began to hit him around the ears again. Arsène was so stunned that he wanted to vomit, as though everything in his head had fallen down into his throat. Bérubé threatened him now, waving his closed fist in front of his eyes.

"Arsène, I'm going to make a good soldier out of you. Tell me exactly what you see when you look in the mirror."

"I see myself."

Bérubé brought back his fist to make him understand that the threat was stronger. "One last time. What do you see in the mirror? "

"I see a pile of shit."

Bérubé had won. He smiled; he hugged Arsène. He patted his cheek. "Now you're a real good soldier."

★ ★ ★ ★ ★

The shouting had awakened Molly. She stretched out her hand to caress Bérubé, but finding that he was not in the bed she started as though she had just awakened from a nightmare. At that moment Bérubé was shouting some blasphemy. Recognizing his voice, she jumped out of bed onto the cold floor, slipped on her dress, which she had let fall on the floor and, worried ran downstairs.

She appeared like another incarnation of the devil, in this house where they were holding a wake for a dead man. In her haste Molly had put on the dress without taking the trouble to put her petticoat on first. She was completely naked because the dress was made of very sheer tulle. No one dared raise his voice to tell her to go and get dressed.

Molly stopped on the stairs for a moment, trying to understand what was going on. She held herself regally under the long transparent gown. The women closed their eyes and imagined that they too were beginning to look like this girl — before the children, the sleepless nights, their husbands' rough words, before those winters, each one more interminable than the last. They would never look like that again; they despised her. The men were devoured by that flame so sweetly sculptured beneath the tulle. A fire was trembling in their bodies. That belly, rounded for caresses, wasn't a swollen sack of guts; those breasts, firm as hot rolls, didn't wobble down onto the belly. The young men put a hand in their pockets and drew their legs close together.

Molly had learned not to get mixed up in men's quarrels. She crossed the kitchen, head held high as though nothing had happened, and went to the living room. There was no reaction, no movement from the soldiers at attention. Molly knelt down before Corriveau's coffin and prayed to God not to condemn to his terrible hell the soul of Corriveau, whom she had never known, but who had such respectable parents. He had been born a French Canadian so he couldn't have been very happy.

Corriveau must have looked like all those young soldiers who used to come to her bed to forget that no one loved them; Molly used to feel very pleased when, after they had got dressed again, they would give her a last kiss, with a certain happiness in their eyes. She liked these young soldiers very much. Their desires were never complicated like those of the old officers or the travelling salesmen who always asked her for all sorts of fancy stuff which she didn't like but which she agreed to because they paid well. Only the young soldiers made her happy. Corriveau would have been like those young soldiers; when he had closed the bedroom door perhaps she would have been sorry to see him leave. Some returned to her bed, and she sometimes recognized them, but there were also some who didn't come back.

Now the young soldiers, the old officers, the travelling salesmen and all the others would never come to her bed again to knead her flesh with avid hands, as though they wanted to model in that flesh another woman's body: the body of the woman they were thinking about. Bérubé alone would love her now.

Molly became very sad at the thought of those young soldiers who would never come again to her bedroom with their affected coarseness, who would never again let an "I love you" escape into her ear at the moment when they were swollen with all their useless love. Molly wiped a tear. All her love would be destined for Bérubé. They would forget her quickly enough: Molly wasn't the only one in the hotel, and there were other hotels. Some of them, of course, could not forget her — the little soldiers who had not come back from the war, who would never come back. If Molly were ever unhappy they would be the ones whose help she would ask. Those little soldiers who had given their lives in the war could not refuse to help Molly. She prayed that God would open the doors of his Heaven to all the young soldiers who looked like Corriveau. She recited several prayers, but is was very difficult. She did not manage to recite them all the way to the end because the desire to sleep was stronger than her desire to save the souls of young war-heroes, stronger than her distress at seeing young men like Corriveau know death before they had known life. It would be better to go to sleep right away. Molly would get up very early, at dawn, well rested. Then she would ask God for the salvation of Corriveau and all those like him.

"Here little girl, little lady, eat this bit of *tourtière*." Mother Corriveau put a plate on Corriveau's coffin in front of Molly, who took a mouthful to be polite.

"You," said Mother Corriveau to the soldiers, "you're not having much fun. Goodness but you look sad. You're soldiers, you shouldn't be sad. You'd think you were in

74

mourning. What if you are Anglais? We don't wish you any harm. We won't send you back home to England. We like you alright. Would you each like a little plate with a piece of *tourtière* like I've given our little Molly? "

The soldiers didn't move. Only the sergeant's eyes turned in their sockets. His lips barely unfastened as he said, "Sorry, we're on duty."

And, to harden his men's positions, he shouted, "Attention! "

Molly nibbled another mouthful and got up to go to bed. When she went into the kitchen Bérubé seized her arm and said to her, "Come here you, all naked, we need your help."

Would Bérubé beat her? She noticed that she was, as her husband had said, really naked under the tulle dress.

Arsène, ludicrously, was standing in front of Bérubé, who kept hitting him with his open hand. Would Bérubé mistreat her like that too? The big man's face was so red that the flesh seemed to want to burst.

"What do you want? " she asked submissively.

Arsène was wearing a buttoned coat; a wool scarf was tied around his neck. Seeing him bundled up like that Molly could not know that under his top coat he was wearing two others.

Arsène did not try to dodge the blows. He was pale, sweaty, suffering.

"Get on his shoulders, get on his back. I don't know how to say it to you. *Baptême*, that language of yours wasn't invented by Christians. Get on his shoulders. That *baptême* is going to learn what a soldier's life is like."

Bérubé seized Molly by the waist, lifted her, and installed her on Arsène's shoulders.

"That's enough," said someone who had come up to

75

them. He couldn't go on: he was silenced by a fist. The man recoiled, surprised at the blood that was running down his chin.

The villagers laughed derisively.

"By Christ, you're going to learn what war's all about. Dance! It isn't finished. Dance! "

Arsène's eyes were burning with sweat. Under his coats his suit was soaked as if a bucket of water, boiling water, had been poured over him. During his lifetime he had carried few things as heavy as little Molly; he'd be crushed by her weight. But he danced so that he wouldn't be hit any more. He would even have kissed Bérubé's feet. He danced with all his strength; his feet were scarcely moving, they were so heavy that when he moved he felt as if he were buried in snow up to his thighs, snow that burned like fire and clung like mud. He would have liked to dance still more so that Bérubé would stop being angry.

"Dance! "

Arsène gathered up all his strength and thought he had speeded up his rhythm.

"Dance, by Christ! Dance! "

Bérubé struck. Molly told herself that she wasn't dreaming.

"Dance faster! "

On Arséne's shoulders Molly looked like a queen. The old men marvelled at the pink tips of her breasts under the tulle, two fascinating little stars. Basically they were no better off than Corriveau. They would never again have the privilege of gently kissing such little pink tips on such tender breasts. They would never again caress such beautiful breasts, all warm in their hands. They were sad. Their lives were over already. And they cursed from the bottoms of their hearts the young men who were devouring Molly with their eyes.

76

"*Allez! Hop! Allez! Hop! Vivent* the soldiers! Go on! Dance, *hostie!* Dance! Faster! Run! *Vive* the army! *Vive la guerre!* Left! Right! Left! Right! Left . . . Left . . . Left . . ."

Bérubé didn't stop Arsène, who was completely under his command.

"Left . . . Left . . . Right! Dance, you stinking vermin! Dance! *Vive la guerre et les soldats!* Dance! Left! Right! Here's a shell! "

Bérubé kicked him in the rear.

"Here's a grenade! "

Bérubé slapped him.

"Here's a bomb! "

Bérubé spat in his face.

"Run! You're rottener than Corriveau will be after the spring thaw. Faster! Left, turn! " Arsène obeyed as well he could. He ran in place, more and more slowly; his face was drowned in sweat. He couldn't breathe. There was a cold stone in place of his lungs. He was stifling. The air was not coming to either his mouth or his nose. He was as thirsty as if he had eaten sand.

"Go on, soldier! Left! Right! Left! Right! Left! Right! Soldier, left turn! "

If Bérubé judged that he was not being obeyed promptly enough, he crushed Arsène's head between his two hands, cracking them over Arsène's ears. Bérubé was as sweaty as Arsène. Molly felt drunk.

"It's lovely, a soldier's life. You would have liked to be a soldier. Look out! It's a mine! "

Bérubé gave him a few kicks on the shin. Hadn't Arsène felt some pain? He showed no reaction, no contortions, no grimaces. He was shaking.

"Ah! the lovely war. Left! Right! *Hostie* of a mule, forward march. Look out! a torpedo! "

Bérubé sank his fist into Arsène's stomach. He was doubled over by the blow. His face was purple. His coats and his wool scarf were strangling him. Would he be strong enough to get up? He was staggering.

No one came to interfere. No one was brave enough. In order not to feel like cowards they tried to be amused, and laughed as they had never laughed before.

"March! "

Arsène felt as if there was a bar of red hot iron in his skull, from one ear to the other. He could no longer see anything; he would have sworn that his eyes were running down his cheeks. What was that flowing, thick and hot, down his temples? Was it sweat or blood? Arsène sank into a deeper and deeper torpor.

"Left! Right! "

Arsène's legs were melting like the pats of butter in Mother Corriveau's saucepans. She was as quiet as she used to be when her son, the one lying there in his coffin, used to come in drunk and insult Anthyme.

Arsène's legs had melted. He was resting now against his fat belly. He could no longer run or dance. He was an exhausted, legless cripple in his soaked coats. Arsène was thinking "I'm plastered, I'm asleep, I've had too much to drink. I'm letting myself fall on the ground."

Bérubé was hitting him. "Left! Right! Left . . . Left! Here's the beautiful life of a little soldier. Look out! Here's a shell! "

Bérubé flattened his hand in Arsène's face.

"When are those Christly Germans going to leave us in peace? " asked Bérubé.

Arsène no longer had any arms. He had become a sack of potatoes, but he still obeyed.

"You're a good soldier. Left! Right! "

On Arsène's shoulders Molly felt humiliated.

Suddenly, Arsène stumbled. Molly fell onto one of the men, who received her in his arms like a flaming log.

"Narcisse! " cried his wife. "Don't touch that! "

Bérubé came up to Arsène, who had passed out on the floor. He stuck his foot in his face and shook his head. "That's a real good little soldier; not as good as Corriveau, but better than me. Arsène is a *Christ* of a good soldier. He deserves medals, stacks of medals as high as churches. Arsène lets himself be pulled apart. He doesn't try to save a single tiny bit of his skin. He's no miser. A *hostie* of a good little soldier."

With his left toe he turned over Arsène's face.

"He'd let them make mincemeat out of him if they told him they needed his skin to plug up the walls of the shithouses. A real good little soldier. But he hasn't got a uniform."

Bérubé pulled off the coats that he had made Arsène pile into, one on top of the other. He took off his jacket, tore off his shirt, which he threw into the woodstove, and pulled off his trousers; the women no longer dared to look. The men were snorting with laughter. Arsène, motionless, submitted to all the outrages. He was nothing but a mass of obedient flesh.

"You're a real good little soldier," said Bérubé, who was no longer pale, whose eyes were no longer haggard. He looked more gentle. "You're a real good little soldier and you've done a goddamn good job for your country, but you've got to have a uniform. It's your duty to fight the war: it's the most glorious job, to fight a war. It's fun to fight a war; it's nice. You're a good soldier, but you haven't got a uniform."

Arsène, dazed, dressed in his long wool underwear

79

that covered him from his ankles to his neck, listened to Bérubé. He repeated, "You need a uniform." The women had an equivocal smile on their lips; the men, their mouths wide open, were amused. Bérubé grabbed hold of the neck of Arsène's underwear, one hand on either side of the long row of buttons that started at the neck and went down to the crotch. Without loosening his grip he pulled, vigorously. Buttons flew, the underwear fell down, Arsène's white chest appeared, then his fat shiny belly. When Arsène, unresisting, was completely naked, the women laughed as hard as their husbands.

Arsène himself burst out laughing.

"Soldier, never forget that your uniform represents your native land, your *patrie* our country, and Liberty."

Bérubé kicked Arsène towards the door and pushed him out into the snow.

"Go on, soldier, go and stomp out three or four goddamn Germans for me."

The villagers gurgled as they emptied themselves of their laughter, and all their insides seemed to escape with their laughter. They held their stomachs, they wept, they stamped their feet, they pranced about, they choked.

Bérubé seized the arm of the astonished Molly.

"Darling," she asked, "why did you do that? "

"What? "

"It was a bad joke."

"Let's go to bed; let's have a little nap."

"Darling . . ."

"Sometimes I feel a little crazy."

★ ★ ★ ★ ★

80

The candles on Corriveau's coffin had burned out. Now the living room was lit only by the light coming from the kitchen. The light was yellow, greasy looking. The soldiers had been present, imperturbable, at Arsène's massacre. They had looked impassively at the savage rites, drowned in heavy laughter, cider and greasy *tourtières,* but their lips were sealed by disgust.

What kind of animals *were* these French Canadians? They had the manners of pigs in a pigpen. Besides, if you looked at them carefully, objectively, French Canadians really looked like pigs too. The long thin Anglais looked at the French Canadians' double chins, their swollen bellies, the big flaccid breasts of their women; they scrutinized the French Canadians' eyes, floating inertly in the white fat of their faces — they were real pigs, these French Canadians, whose civilization consisted of drinking, eating, farting, belching. The soldiers had known for a long time that French Canadians were pigs. "Give them something to eat and a place to shit and we'll have peace in the country," they used to say. That night the soldiers had proof before their eyes that the French Canadians were pigs.

Corriveau, the French Canadian they had transported on their shoulders through snow so deep it made them want to stretch out and freeze they were so tired, Corriveau, this French Canadian sleeping under their flag, in a uniform like the one they were so proud of, this Corriveau was a pig too.

French Canadians were pigs. Where would it end? The sergeant decided that it was time to take the situation in hand. French Canadians were unmanageable, undisciplined, crazy pigs. The sergeant prepared a plan of attack in his head.

His subalterns remembered what they had learned in

school: French Canadians were solitary, fearful, barely intelligent; they didn't have a talent for government or business or agriculture, but they made lots of babies.

When the English arrived in the colony the French Canadians were less civilized than the Indians. The French Canadians lived grouped in little villages along the shores of the St. Lawrence, in wooden cabins filled with dirty, sick, starving children, and lousy, dying old men. Every year English ships used to go up the St. Lawrence because England had decided to get involved in New France, which had been neglected and abandoned by the Frenchmen. The English ships were anchored in front of the villages, and the Englishmen got off to offer their protection to the French Canadians, to become friends with them. But as soon as they had seen the British flag waving on the St. Lawrence the French Canadians had gone and hidden in the woods. Real animals. They hadn't a vestige of politeness, these pigs. They didn't even think of defending themselves. What they left behind — their cabins, animals, furniture, clothes — were so dirty, so crawling with vermin, so smelly, that the English had had to burn it all in order to disinfect the area. If they hadn't destroyed it the vermin would have invaded the whole country.

Then the boats went away, but the French Canadians stayed in the woods until autumn. Then they got busy building new cabins.

Why did they not accept the help offered by the English? Because France had abandoned them, why would they not accept the privilege of becoming English? England would have civilized them. They wouldn't be French-Canadian pigs then. They would know how to understand a civilized language. They would speak a civilized language, not a *patois*.

Accustomed to obeying, the soldiers felt that they were being given an order. They turned their eyes towards the sergeant, who motioned with his head. The soldiers understood. They carried out the order fervently.

They went through the house picking up boots, coats, scarves and hats, and threw them outside. The villagers were invited to leave.

More preoccupied with finding their clothes than protesting the insult, they left, pushing each other as they went.

★ ★ ★ ★ ★

When they were outside, their feet buried in snow crusted from the same cold that froze the saliva on their lips, the villagers realized that they had been kicked out of Corriveau's house by the Anglais. The Anglais had prevented them from praying for the repose of the soul of Corriveau, a boy from the village, dead in the war, the Anglais' war. Their humiliation was as painful as a physical wound. The Anglais were preventing them from gathering together to mourn at the coffin of one of their people. Because life in the village was lived in common, each villager was Corriveau's father to some extent, each woman his mother. The women wept bitterly; the men held in their anger. Gradually they all found their clothes. They were not cold now: their anger protected them from the wind.

Mother Corriveau had not liked the soldiers' behaviour, but she couldn't communicate with them in their language. She put some wood in the stove. "You have to hit these Anglais over the head to make them understand."

Anthyme didn't say whether he agreed or not. Mother Corriveau, without saying another word, indicated to the Anglais that they should sit down at the table, where she served them generous portions of *tourtière* swimming in fragrant sauce.

Father Anthyme didn't want his cider drunk by these Anglais who had kicked out the people who had come to pray for his son. But he went down to his cellar and dug up some more bottles. "We know how to live," he said to the soldiers, who smiled because they didn't understand a word.

★ ★ ★ ★ ★

Henri, the deserter, in order not to risk being caught and taken back to the army by the Anglais soldiers, remained under cover in his attic, motionless in his bed, while Amélie and Arthur went out to pray for Corriveau's salvation. Henri breathed carefully, avoiding any movement, any creaking of his old mattress that could reveal, in this too perfect silence, the presence of a man who refused to go to war.

Henri even had to force his children and those of his wife — that is, the ones she had had with Arthur — to forget about him.

The presence in the village of those seven soldiers who had accompanied Corriveau gave him palpitations; the soldiers could very well go back with their hands not empty: there were a number of deserters in the village. Because Amélie wanted to live with two men in the house Henri would be one of the first to be captured. The people in the village didn't like two men living with the same woman. Henri knew he was superfluous. It wouldn't take the soldiers long to find him if they looked.

He despised his fear as he despised himself for having lost Amélie. Even if he had his turn in bed with her, even if she called him when Arthur went out, Henri was well aware that she preferred Arthur.

Under his skin, in his flesh, the smarting of his anguish tormented him; he wanted to scratch himself, to claw until the blood came. He would not forgive himself for hiding away in a glacial attic, a man whose wife had been taken away from him and who was afraid that they would come to this black hole where he was scared, where he despised himself, and force him to go back to the war.

The sun had set very early as it always does in winter, when even the light does not resist the cold. But despite the invading night Henri did not sleep.

In all fairness, it was his turn to sleep with Amélie tonight, but because of Corriveau he would lose it. He didn't dare let himself be seen on the outside. Amélie had had Arthur go along with her to see Corriveau. Suddenly it occurred to Henri that it was just as dangerous for Arthur to go out and be seen by the seven soldiers as it was for him, because Arthur was as much a deserter as he was. In fact, Arthur was even more of a criminal because he had never even worn a uniform. Because he was going to pray with Amélie, Arthur had insisted on spending the night in her bed. Henri had had the wool pulled over his eyes once too often. He despised himself. Perhaps Amélie and Arthur would give themselves up to the soldiers? Henri flattened himself into his bed and pulled the covers over his head. Arthur would spend two consecutive nights with Amélie while Henri, in his attic, was bored to death.

Every night he was tortured by the same thought: his wife no longer belonged to him, his house no longer belonged to him, nor his animals, not even his children, who all called Arthur "papa." He cursed the war; he gathered up all the curses he knew, inventing some that came from the bottom of his heart, and loosed them against the war. He hated the war with all his heart. But he thought sometimes that he would be less unhappy in the mud of the war. It even seemed to him more desirable to be unhappy with his family, in his own house, than to be happy in the war. Then he would tell himself that it was better to be unhappy in a cold attic than happy in the mud of the war. But he knew above all that man is unhappy wherever he is, that in the village the only man who was not unhappy was Corriveau, on condition that there was no hell and no purgatory. Drowned in the untidy remorse of his thoughts, Henri fell asleep.

Shortly after, he awoke, thinking of the sun. The thought of the sun had awakened him just like a real ray of sunlight caressing your face on a summer morning.

Henri's sun was only a mirage, a poor thought that would not revive the dead earth beneath the ice and snow, an idea that would not light up the attic where Henri feared the night and the mysterious shadows. He pulled the covers over his head again to give himself the illusion of warmth and security. Henri's sun would not even light up the sad recesses of his mind.

Henri had dreamed of a big sun, round as an orange; he could still see it in his mind, precise, high, immense, dizzily motionless. He imagined it was suspended by a wire; if the wire were cut the sun would fall and, opening its mouth, it would swallow the whole world. Henri contemplated this sun. There was nothing above it or beside it. It was indeed a solitary sun.

Henri noticed that, beneath this sun, something was arranging itself on the ground. It looked like a house, but as he observed more carefully he saw that it was not a house but a big box, and as he thought better he realized that it was Corriveau's coffin, which he had seen going by in the street covered with the Anglais' flag. Henri saw the sun, then, very high, and on the earth he could see nothing but Corriveau's coffin.

To tell the truth, this coffin beneath the sun was bigger than Corriveau's, because the people from the village were entering it, one by one, one after the other, just as they entered church, bent over, submissive, and the last villagers brought their animals with them — cows, horses, and the others following. It was a silent cortège. The coffin was much more vast than the village church for, as well as the villagers and their animals, squirrels, snakes, dogs and foxes were entering the coffin; even the river suddenly climbed up like a snake to enter the coffin. Birds came down from the sky to go into it, and people from neighbouring villages. The cortège was interrupted; people were arriving with their baggage and their children and their animals. Henri was among these strangers, and he went into the coffin too. Houses were moving like awkward turtles; covered with ice and snow they slid along heavily and disappeared into Corriveau's coffin. Now people were arriving in crowds, whole villages at a time, huge numbers of people patiently waiting their turn. They came in trains, hundreds of trains, then giant steamboats drew up and spilled their crowds into Corriveau's coffin. From the four corners of the earth people came running up, rushing into Corriveau's coffin which was swelling up like a stomach. The sea too, even the sea had become gentle as a river and was emptying itself into Corriveau's coffin: he saw fish with eight hands, with three heads, crabs with terrifying teeth, insects too, creatures in shells that seemed like pebbles, then nothing more. The entire ocean had been drunk up and in the whole world nothing remained but Corriveau's coffin.

"Now it's all over," thought Henri.

The earth was deserted. Now the coffin seemed very small, hardly as big as the one Henri had seen going by on the shoulders of the Anglais soldiers. The earth was silent, motionless. Henri was relieved not to be thinking of anything.

Then groups of men, mechanically disciplined, began spilling out from the torn horizon. They were soldiers, armed, marching in step. Countless armies were marching towards one another; their march was fierce, implacable. Henri understood that they would converge at Corriveau's coffin. They did not raise their weapons but, soldierlike, entered Corriveau's coffin. Henri waited a long time. Nothing more happened. On the whole earth, only Corriveau's coffin under the Anglais flag still existed.

He cried to himself, "I'm going crazy! " He moaned again, "I'm losing my mind! "

He sat up in his bed. Night was over and day had begun in his attic. Henri noticed Corriveau's coffin. It was in his attic. Henri saw it, at the back of the attic. A hand was pushing Henri's back, pushing him towards Corriveau's coffin which now was just big enough to contain one man:

Corriveau or himself.

"Help!"

He leapt from his bed, pushed aside the trunks, lifted the trapdoor, let himself down and ran downstairs. The children were asleep; the walls were cracking as though the devil was nibbling at them.

Henri slipped into Arthur's boots, put on his wool jacket and his fur cap. Despite the danger of being caught by the soldiers and taken back to the war, Henri decided to join the others at Corriveau's house. The door was open: he hesitated on the step.

The night was so black, the village so flooded by the night, it seemed so deep that Henri felt dizzy.

He stuck the shotgun in his hand.

When the villagers found themselves in front of Anthyme Corriveau's house, their feet in the snow which was as sharp as splinters of glass, when they understood that they had been expelled from Anthyme Corriveau's house, that they had been thrown out into this icy sea where they were trembling in their soaking clothes, when they thought again that it was outsiders, Anglais, who had chased them out of Corriveau's house, a house that had come down through five generations of Corriveaus, all living in the village and in the same house on the same bit of land for more than a hundred years; when they reminded themselves that Corriveau, a little French-

89

Canadian boy, a son of the village, had been killed in a war that the Anglais from England, the United States and Canada had declared on the Germans (Corriveau had been killed in the mud of the old country while the Anglais were sitting on cushions in their offices; the Anglais left their shelters sometimes, but only to go and bring a young French Canadian, dead in the war, back to his family); when the villagers realized that they had been sent out like dogs that had peed on the rug by the Anglais who weren't from their village or their county or their province, or even their country, Anglais who weren't even Canadians but only *maudits* Anglais then the villagers knew the depth of their humiliation.

Gesticulating, swearing, bickering, arguing, pushing and shoving, spitting, drunk, they swore inflammatory oaths agains the Anglais who had settled themselves into Corriveau's house.

Joseph waved his stump, wrapped up in its bandages, and shouted louder than the others. "The *maudits* Anglais have taken everything away from us, but they haven't got our Corriveau. They won't get Corriveau's last night! "

★ ★ ★ ★ ★

Sweat was streaming over the body of little Mireille, over her face, and wetting the sheets.

She didn't move.

She couldn't stir; her limbs refused. The night weighed on her like the stories of the loaded wagon that

90

had capsized on her the summer before. Only her eylids were moving. She opened her eyes, then closed them. Though her eyes were shut she could still see.

Mireille wished that she could see nothing.

She raised her foot and looked at it as though it wasn't hers, as though there was only her foot in the bedroom.

In the light Mireille could see her toes at the end of her foot. She curled them, uncurled them, and watched them move. Then she stopped. She saw her foot as it really was: it was wax. She could no longer shake her wax toes, she could no longer pivot her foot around her ankle. She didn't dare touch her wax foot, even with her fingertips.

She wanted to yell, but she had lost her voice. She couldn't call for help.

Mireille especially did not think of her fear. She was busy instead watching the smile of Corriveau who was lying in her little brother's place.

Mireille had seen Corriveau sometimes when he was still in the village, and today she had seen his cortège go by.

Corriveau was smiling.

Mireille knew that Corriveau would get up. She waited, stiff, paralysed, mute. She waited dutifully. Then Mireille heard the sound of the straw in the mattress. She saw Corriveau get up, look in the pockets of his trousers and take out a match. He lit it with his thumbnail. He looked around him. Then he walked towards Mireille's feet, lighting his way with the match.

Corriveau brought the match near Mireille's foot. She saw little flames start up at the end of her wax foot.

Satisfied, Corriveau went back to lie down in the coffin, which was in the place of her brother's bed.

Corriveau lay down, stretched out with satisfaction, and fell asleep smiling.

Mireille was suffocating. But she could do nothing with her toes, those ten little burning candles that were watching over Corriveau.

★ ★ ★ ★ ★

Anthyme Corriveau and his wife had fed the Anglais as though they were boys from the village. They watched them. The Anglais ate little. They spoke little. They drank little. If one of the Anglais spoke, the others were quiet and listened. If a question were asked one at a time would answer. They didn't laugh: instead, they compressed their lips in a miserly smile. Anthyme and his wife could not understand what the Anglais were saying, but they didn't like to hear the sounds of their language because of their eyes. "Their eyes aren't frank," thought Anthyme. They had the impression that the Anglais were making fun of them when they spoke.

"We're all French Canadians here," thought Father Corriveau; "my little boy who is dead is a French Canadian, everyone is a French Canadian. The whole province is French Canadian, there are French all across Canada, even in the United States. So why did they send these Anglais to bring back my son? "

Anthyme Corriveau could not overcome a certain sadness; it was not because he had lost his child, but another sorrow that he couldn't explain.

Listening to her rattling saucepans in the sink the old man knew that his wife was not pleased with the way things had worked out.

"We were among our own people, all from the village," she was thinking. "We all knew each other, because we all live the same life; we raise our children together. My son is the son of the whole village. All the people who were here are a little bit his parents and I could even say that the young people were his brothers or sisters. Even when trouble comes to the village we like to be together; we all share the trouble, and then it's not so hard to bear. When we're all together we're stronger, and the trouble doesn't bother us as much. Why did the Anglais break up our get-together? My son would have been happy to see us all around him. But the Anglais have broken up our evening. I'll remember it for the rest of my life."

Mother Corriveau didn't want to serve the Anglais at the table any more. She offered them three or four *tourtières* and went into the living room. Anthyme put a bottle of cider on the table and found his wife kneeling in front of their son's coffin.

In the kitchen the Anglais were speaking in low voices, saying words that Mother Corriveau and her husband could no longer take the trouble to understand. Hands joined on the coffin, Anthyme Corriveau and his wife forgot about the Anglais whose voices came to them discreet, distant. The old couple were alone. It was the first time they had been alone with their son. They were close to each other as they had been on their wedding day. Mother Corriveau was wiping away tears as she had on that day. Anthyme's eyes would not permit tears but, as on his wedding day, he had a violent desire to cry, to swear, to hit himself, to break something. Had they lived their lives to come to this dismay, this sorrow?

The paths of everyone's lives, they were thinking, lead to the coffin. They could only accept that this law was a fair one. She wept. He raged. Mother Corriveau did not want life to be like this. Anthyme could not remake it, but he was convinced that if it was necessary for coffins to go by, and for life to stop at a coffin, it was not fair for people to have such an obvious love of life.

The old people wept.

What was the use of having been a child with blue eyes, of having learned about life, its names, its colours, its laws, painfully as though it were against nature? What was the use of having been a child so unlucky in life? What was the use of the prayers of that pious child, who had been as pale as the pictures of the Saints? What was the use of the blasphemies of the child become a man?

Everything was as useless as tears.

What was the use then of the sleepless nights that Mother Corriveau had spent consoling the child who cried from the pain of living? What was the use of the old people's grief?

Anthyme could not stay on his knees. He wanted to destroy something. He went to the stove, took some logs, and threw them on the fire. Mother Corriveau wiped her tears with her apron.

"God isn't reasonable."

She wanted to say that he was exaggerating, that he was not being fair. Anthyme came back to her. "It's not worth the trouble to have children if God does that," he said, indicating his son.

His wife thought of the others: Albéric, Ferdinand, Toussaint, Gaston, Alonzo, and Anatole who were in countries where they were fighting the war against the Germans. There was even Ernest and Nazaire in countries where they were fighting the Japanese. They were shooting bullets at this moment, without knowing that their brother had been killed. Mother Corriveau realized that it was night; no, right now her children were not fighting: they were asleep, because it was night. The thought reassured her. When would they learn that their brother was dead? Would they know before the war was over? Letters arrived at their destinations so seldom.

Suddenly, Mother Corriveau got up. An image had come to her, terrifying, an image to make her die of grief. She had seen in her mind the coffins of all her boys piled up one on top of another.

"Anthyme! Anthyme! " she begged.

He started. "What is it? "

She ran to him in tears, pressed herself against him. Anthyme's arms closed around her.

"We have to say a lot of prayers."

"I'm going to the barn. I want to swear.'"

★ ★ ★ ★ ★

Joseph-with-the-hand-cut-off was the first to dash towards the house. The others followed. He smashed into the door. The house shook as if a bull had fallen on the roof. The windows trembled. The door sprang open as if someone had pulled it. Joseph brandished his stump in its bloody rags. "We want our Corriveau! We want our

95

Corriveau! You're not taking our Corriveau! "

Anthyme went to Joseph calmly. "Cut off your hands, cut off your feet too if you want, cut off your neck if that's what you want, but don't tear out my doors! "

Mother Corriveau stayed beside her husband, an iron pot in her hand, ready to strike. "I've just taken it off the fire, and it's red hot. I'll fry your face, you with the hand cut off."

The Anglais had got up politely as the villagers came in. Plates were broken on the floor, glasses too. Threats were shouted: "You won't get our Corriveau! Go back to England, *maudits Anglais de calice!* There's a train at noon tomorrow; take it and don't come back! "

A woman remarked, "He's cute, the little one there. Too bad he's an Anglais."

"A *Christ* of an Anglais," her husband specified, kicking her in the ankle as punishment.

"They aren't even real Anglais. They came to Canada because the real Anglais in England wanted to get rid of them."

"You're not taking our Corriveau! "

"Our Corriveau belongs to us! "

The villagers fought over the Anglais. Each of them wanted to catch one. When an Anglais was taken over by two or three villagers they shook him, pulled his moustache, flicked their fingers against his ears. The soldiers grimaced with disgust as they received right in their faces the alcoholic breath coming out of these French Canadians. They barely defended themselves. The villagers spun the soldiers around like tops. They staggered. The villagers pulled their neckties; shirt buttons went flying. The women amused themselves by groping at the Anglais' trousers; each time they found what they were looking for

96

they chortled, "He's got one! "

Then the sergeant cried, "Let's go boys! Let's kill 'em! "

The soldiers obeyed, attacking men and women. The villagers redoubled their violence and their anger. The Anglais defended themselves with their fists or their boots, their big leather boots; they struck out at faces, at stomachs, at teeth; faces were bloody; they trampled over bodies stretched out on the floor, crushed fingers, and fought with plates and chairs.

"You're not getting our Corriveau! "

"Let's kill 'em! Let's kill 'em! "

Mouths were spitting blood.

"*Christ de calice de tabernacle!* "

"*Maudit wagon de Christ à deux rangées de bancs, deux Christs par banc!* "

"*Saint-Chrême d'Anglais!* "

"We're going to get our Corriveau! "

Bérubé appeared in the stairway again, barefoot, bare-chested, in his trousers. The uproar and the shouting had wakened him. He looked over the situation. He understood that the soldiers were fighting against the villagers. He jumped over the stairs. He wanted to smash some Anglais jaws. He'd show these Anglais what a French Canadian had in his fist.

"Attention! " shouted an English voice. Bérubé was paralysed by these words. The sergeant had given an order: Bérubé, simple soldier, was hypnotised.

"Let's kill 'em! "

These words brought Bérubé back to life. The soldier without rank obeyed as he knew how. He struck out at the villagers as though his life were in danger. He had to hit harder than the people from the village and harder than

97

the Anglais if he wanted anyone to respect him.

Little by little the villagers lost the battle. Bloody, burning with fever, humiliated, disgusted, swearing, they went after each other, and one after the other they came to, defeated, their heads in the snow.

Outside, the villagers continued to threaten. "You're not getting our Corriveau! "

The sergeant ordered the Anglais and Bérubé to go out and end the brawl.

Under the gray light of the moon, in the cold air that seemed to be bursting into pieces like a thin skin of ice, the little war refused to be extinguished. It calmed down, then all at once burst out again, on all sides. People were twisted with pain, groaning, swearing, weeping with impotence.

Suddenly, a shot — dry, like the crack of a whip.

★ ★ ★ ★ ★

Henri had run towards Anthyme's house, pursued by Corriveau's coffin which was following him through the night like a starving dog.

A soldier appeared before him. He thought the soldier wanted to arrest him and take him back to the war.

He fired.

The scuffle was over. The Anglais picked up the wounded man, carried him into the house and laid him out on the kitchen table. The soldier was dead.

The Anglais carried the table and the soldier into the

living room, across from Corriveau's coffin.

"It's very sad," said Mother Corriveau; "I have no more candles.

★ ★ ★ ★ ★

Everyone got down on their knees. The Anglais prayed in their language for their compatriot. The villagers prayed in French Canadian for their Corriveau. Bérubé didn't know whether he should pray in English for the Anglais or in French Canadian for Corriveau. He started to recite the words of a prayer he had learned in school. "*Au fond tu m'abimes, Seigneur, Seigneur . . .*"

He didn't go on. The villagers were looking at him with hatred, the hatred they felt for a traitor. Because he had fought with the Anglais against the people of his village, Bérubé had become an Anglais to them. He didn't have the right to pray for Corriveau: their hard looks told him that. So Bérubé decided to pray in English. "My Lord! Thou . . ."

The Anglais turned towards him. In their eyes Bérubé read that they would not tolerate a French Canadian praying for an Anglais. Bérubé left.

Several bottles of cider were abandoned on the floor, open. He grabbed one and drank it. The cider gurgled, poured down his cheeks onto his chest. Then he went up to the bedroom where Molly was sleeping, threw his clothes across the room, tore off the covers, and threw himself onto Molly, without even bothering to wake her up.

"*Ma ciboire d'Anglaise*. I'll show you what a French Canadian is."

She dreamed that a knife was tearing her stomach open. She started. Then, reassured, she pretended to be asleep.

Bérubé grew agitated, frantic; he sweated, whimpered, kissed, embraced. He hated.

"Those *crucifix d'Anglais* sleep all the time. No wonder they have such small families. And when the Anglais make a war they come and look for the French Canadians."

Bérubé had spoken out loud. Molly understood. She smiled. Slowly, she caressed his back. He shivered.

"That *ciboire* will be the death of me . . ."

Molly mocked him. "Are you asleep, darling? "

★ ★ ★ ★ ★

Some of the villagers felt an urgent need for sleep. They lay down three or four to a bed, or on the braided rugs, or on the bare floor, or a fur coat. Several were sitting in chairs, another was on his knees before Corriveau and the Anglais. But most got through the night as though it had been daylight. The night passed quite peacefully. They chatted, exchanged memories, repeated the adventures that are always told on such occasions, counted the people who had disappeared, recalled Corriveau's deeds and gestures, ate *tourtières,* drank cider, prayed, pinched a passing bottom, made up stories, choked with laughter, and went back to their prayers, the tears coming to their eyes: such injustice to die at Corriveau's age while suffering old people were begging the Lord to call them to him. They blew their noses, wiped their foreheads, cursed the war, prayed God that the Germans would not come to destroy their village, asked Mother Corriveau for another piece of *tourtière*, reasurred Henri who was desperate at having killed a soldier. "It was a case of legitimate self-defence. Have a drink! War's war." The women were sad to see their dresses in such a pitiful state.

The soldiers kneeling by their colleague dead at his duty were so attentive to their prayers that God himself seemed to be at their side.

"*Vieille pipe de Christ!* " said Anthyme. "Those damn protestants know how to pray as well as the French Canadians! "

Mother Corriveau announced that the time had come to form the cortège and go to mass and the burial of her son.

Henri watched over the soldier he had struck down. The others followed Corriveau's coffin, carried on the shoulders of the Anglais and of Bérubé, whose services had been requisitioned.

Henri was afraid. He had deserted because he didn't like the idea of death, and now he was obliged to keep company with a dead man, a dead man killed by Henri himself. He was not afraid of punishment. That was war. During a war you are not punished for killing. Henri was quite happy that the Anglais had not attacked him in peacetime: then, Henri would have been punished.

He saw his body swinging at the end of a rope, suspended from a scaffold planted in the snow that went on as far as the eye could see, and his body had become an icicle; if someone had touched it his body would have tinkled and broken into splinters. Henri was cold; the wind whistled as it moved a dry dust that came to brush against his body, oscillating at the end of its rope. Henri was cold; he buttoned the sweater he had borrowed from Arthur.

It was the idea of being hung from a rope over the snow in the cold that made him tremble: it was a cold fear. He was afraid of this house where he had a dead man for company. He laid his shotgun across his knees. He did not want to pray for the Anglais. He kept quiet, waiting.

The wind was trying to take off the roof. Nails were crackling, beams were twisting and whining. Like a child, Henri was afraid to be alone with this wintry music. He wished that there was someone with him. Then he would not have been afraid. In fact, he did have someone with him, but it was a dead man and that made Henri ten times more alone. With a live companion Henri could have talked, shared some tobacco. But a dead man doesn't talk or smoke.

Henri listened. "What does a dead man think about under his white sheets? Does he hate the person that killed him? A dead man, if he's damned like this *vierge* of a protestant, does he burn inside before he's buried? Dead men get mad at the living. It's the dead who put the fires of hell into barns; you often see it: a house that bursts into flames all of a sudden, without reason, that's hellfire.

There are dead men who walk in the walls of houses too. We cheer ourselves up and say it's winter that's making the houses whine, but it's dead men . . . As long as we haven't prayed enough to rescue their souls from purgatory, the dead come back to earth begging for prayers, and if we don't understand they spread trouble to make us think about them."

Was it Corriveau climbing around in the walls?

Henri tightened his grip on the rifle. He wouldn't fire at the soul of a French Canadian. He wasn't afraid of Corriveau's soul.

But the Anglais . . . perhaps the Anglais would take advantage of his death to revenge himself for not succeeding in wiping out the French Canadians. Henri tightened his grip again: he was ready to shoot.

"If he comes I'll let him have a bullet right through the heart."

All the beams in the house were whining. Henri remembered an evening when he had been lost in the forest. Everything was so damp that it was impossible to light a fire. A soft, heavy wind had come up. Trees, big hundred-year-old spruce, waved their arms and sang like so many souls in distress. Afterwards, Henri did not know if it was trees he had heard or souls.

Perhaps it would calm his imagination if he stared fixedly at the Anglais. When you see someone motionless in front of you you know he isn't moving. A dead man doesn't move.

He was reassured. He was no longer afraid. The Anglais under his sheet was as well-behaved as a stick of wood. Even if all of a sudden the sheet moved, Henri was not afraid. He was not afraid because it was winter, and the wind could come in through a crack in the window, strong enough to make the sheet Mother Corriveau had thrown over the Anglais tremble.

The sheet lifted, and some hair emerged. Henri fired. He was out of the house already, running in the snow. Henri had killed the Corriveau's cat.

★ ★ ★ ★ ★

The priest was talking. When he opened his mouth his tongue looked like a toad that did not dare to jump.

"Veni, vidi, vici, Caesar wrote; Caesar, who like Corriveau, this boy of our parish, practised the most noble profession of arms — that most noble profession after the profession of holiness that is practised by your priests. It was of a military truth that he was speaking. If he had spoken of a human truth Caesar would have written veni, vidi, mortuus sum: I came, I saw, I died.

"My brothers, never forget that we live to die and we die to live.

"The short time of life on earth, this short time is far too long because we have enough time to damn ourselves several times over. Let us be careful that one day Christ does not get tired of wiping out, of washing our consciences; let us be careful that, seeing the deluge of our sins, he does not spill on your heads, my brothers, the fires of hell, just as he spilled on them, through the hand of his priest, the holy waters of baptism. Perhaps the war, at this moment, is a little like the fires of hell that God is pouring over the old countries which are known for their disbelief in the teachings of the Church.

"Life on earth is far too long for many of the faithful who damn themselves for all eternity. Even some of my dear parishioners have been damned, are damning themselves and will walk for all eternity on the poisonous snakes of hell, on the scorpions of hell (they look like little lobsters, but there are big ones too, and they bite); their bodies will be filled with leprosy, the leprosy of sin as it can be seen in pagan countries; they will wander, these damned souls, through all eternity in flames that burn without consuming.

"That is why we must bless God for having come among us to seek the soul of our young Corriveau who, since he is dead, will no longer offend God and the saints. Our son Corriveau, after a life that only God can judge — but God is a fair judge and pitiless, punishing the wicked and rewarding the good — our son Corriveau, dead in a holy way, fighting the war against the Germans.

"My brothers, this black catafalque you see before you and under which our son Corriveau has been placed, you will all enter it one day as Corriveau has entered it today. For you as for him the six torches of the angels of the catafalque will be lit, symbolising the flames that purify the sinner, these flames to which you will submit because of your sinful voluptuous nature. You will submit to the flames of hell if you do not live like the angels who carry them. Do not lose sight, my brothers, of this holy symbol of the church.

"Because you are men and women, because the flesh is weak, you are condemned to perish in the flames of hell, to perish without perishing unless God in his infinite goodness forgives your offences.

"My brothers, every day of your lives, think, think

several times a day, that this catafalque that you will all come to will be the gate of hell if you do not have a perfect contrition for your faults, even for your venial faults, for God, all-powerful and immensely perfect, could not tolerate even a venial imperfection.

"If you were in Corriveau's place this morning, Corriveau who died like a saint defending his religion against the devil disguised as Germans, would you be saved?

"I, your priest, to whom God has given the privilege of knowing, through holy confession, the most intimate secrets of your consciences, I know, God permits me to know that there are several among you, blasphemers, immodest, fornicators, violators of God's sixth commandment which forbids sins of the flesh, drunkards, and you, women, who refuse the children that God would give you, women who are not happy with the ten children God has entrusted to you, and who refuse to have others, women who threaten by your weakness the future of our Catholic faith on this continent; I know that without Christ, who dies every day on the altar when I celebrate the holy mass, I know that you would be damned.

"Let us pray together for the conversion of our sheep who have strayed . . ."

Mother Corriveau was weeping; it was true, then that her son was saved!

★ ★ ★ ★ ★

106

Arsène was also the gravedigger. For him a death in the village was a gift from God, because he sold a pig to the stricken family and also dug a grave. For a long time now his son, Philibert, had been helping him with his work.

As a child, Philibert used to follow his father with his little shovel on his shoulder as he went to the cemetery. Arsène was proud of the child. "I'll make a good worker out of him." At this time Philibert was so small he could not get out of the grave by himself. Arsène would hoist him up in his arms, laughing. At times he would amuse himself by leaving the boy alone in the grave, pretending to abandon him there. In the pit the child would cry, calling to his father until he seemed about to burst. Arsène would not answer: he was seeing to other tasks. When he came back Philibert would often be asleep. Arsène picked up a handful of wet earth and threw it in his face. The child woke up, bewildered.

"So, lazybones, asleep on the job?"

Arsène would bend over the grave, hold out his arms, lift up the child. He leaped to his father's neck and kissed him, furiously. Arsène replied, "A real female, this little *baptême;* affectionate."

It was of such good times past that Arsène was thinking as Philibert declared, from the bottom of the grave, "This ground is frozen like Christ's shit."

Hearing him, Arsène brandished his shovel and threatened him. "You little foulmouth, I'll teach you to have some respect for holy things."

He stuck his shovel in the ground, came up to his son, and sunk his boot in the boy's behind. The blow was painless because Philibert was used to it. He turned to his father calmly, "I'm not defending myself because you're my father, but every time you kick me I think how I'm itching to dig *your* grave."

These words shook Arsène more than a blow from a fist. For a moment, he was stunned. Arsène was no longer the father of a child, but of a man. Philibert had become a man. Time had certainly passed quickly.

"You're right, son. The ground is as hard as frozen *Saint-Chrême*."

"The ground is as hard as a knot in the wood of the crucifix."

"It's as hard as the Pope's mattress."

At each oath father and son bent over with laughter in the grave they had almost finished digging. If they had not had the walls of the grave for support they would have collapsed, they were laughing so hard.

"Son, listen to me. Now you're a man. You know how to talk like a man. Listen to me. Because you're a man I promise never to boot you up the ass again, except in special circumstances."

"Am I really a man? "

"Don't be so innocent — you think I haven't noticed you're like a little stallion in the spring? "

"It's true that I'm a man? *Hostie de tabernacle*, that's good news! "

"Yes, my boy, it's good news! "

Shivering with joy, Philibert jumped out of the grave. Standing on the earth that had been dug up he turned to Arsène. "*Mon vieux Christ* if I'm a man I'm getting the hell out. You can bury yourself all alone! "

"Little *Calvaire*! " roared his father.

They had to finish digging the grave. The earth was hard, chalky.

"Independent little bugger! At noon when you come

to ask for your piece of meat I'll give you a boot in the ass. You're going to learn what life's all about! "

Philibert walked through the snow toward the station. He had decided that he would never come back to the house.

"If I'm a man I'm going to be a soldier like Corriveau."

Arsène went on digging. It was hard to loosen the earth. The pick scarcely bit into it. Arsène hurried.

The first few times he had done this work he had made a notch in the handle of his shovel for every villager who was buried. Now he no longer counted them. There was only a little bit of dirt left to remove, and all he thought of was that little bit of dirt. "This ground is so hard that Corriveau will stay fresh till late spring."

★ ★ ★ ★ ★

Elsewhere in the world there was night, war. Harami, come to study commercial law in Europe, had been sent out to the backwash of the war.

His duty was to sleep for several hours in his wet, muddy sleeping bag so that he would be rested for the call that would sound in a few hours. He did not sleep. He was desperate.

Distant gunshots.

So many men had died beside him and everywhere in Europe and elsewhere, Harami had so often seen guts bursting out of an open belly, he had seen so many men drowned in the mud, he had seen so many limbs torn off, strewn over the ground like demented plants.

Harami thought of a man he had seen die, a new man, arrived that very day. Harami had found himself beside the new man at supper. He had asked a question that Harami had not understood. Then the new one had spoken English with a very heavy accent. "Are you a real nigger from Africa? "

Harami had been offended by the insolence of the question. "No," he had replied, with the unctuous politeness he had picked up in London.

"Is there snow where you come from? "

"In the mountains, yes, there is snow."

"*Bon Dieu de Christ*," exclaimed the new one, "there's so much snow in my village maybe that means I was living on a mountain too."

Harami had smiled.

"They probably haven't got any real toilets here," sneered Corriveau.

"The w.c.'s over there," Harami indicated.

"You've got to line up, wait your turn. I can't."

"Go over there, then, behind the hedge."

"Thanks."

The new one ran, undoing his belt. He disappeared behind the hedge. Harami heard a loud detonation: a mine. A cloud of earth was raised. Harami ran.

Once again there were several shreds of flesh, several bloody bits of clothing, a billfold. By reading the papers Harami had learned Corriveau's name.

★ ★ ★ ★ ★

110

As they were leaving the church they saw the sky, very high, distant, deep as the sea where icebergs would be adrift, because the clouds were white and hard under the sky; when they lowered their eyes the snow was spread out like a sea too, as vast as the sky and the water.

The soldiers who were carrying Corriveau's coffin closed their eyes because the snow reflected the light so brightly that it hurt their eyes, tired from the night's watch. Mother Corriveau, in tears, was leaning with all her weight on the arm of her husband, who was not weeping but who kept repeating that it was he who was being carried to the grave. Behind the old parents of the dead boy they had left a space for the members of the family who had not been able to come to the funeral. Then the villagers followed, silently, this one of their own whom they were about to render unto heaven and to earth.

The clock struck, marking the steps of the cortège. The slowness was infinitely sad.

Little by little Corriveau was forgotten, they were so taken up with hating the snow in which they were hobbling around, and which was melting in their boots and shoes.

Finally they arrived, covered with snow, out of breath, wet and shivering.

The soldiers placed the coffin on the two planks thrown across the grave. They held themselves rigid at the sergeant's order.

"Atten . . . shun! ! ! "

The villagers were arranged in a circle around the grave.

The sergeant brought his bugle to his mouth, puffed out his cheeks, and blew. The very earth wept under the snow. From the depths of their memories of Corriveau alive, the tears came. Those who did not want to cry choked. In her wedding dress Molly wept beside Anthyme Corriveau and his wife. Only the eyes of the soldiers were dry.

★ ★ ★ ★ ★

Then, holding the coffin by cables they let slip between their hands, the soldiers lowered Corriveau into his grave.

Arsène prepared to throw the first pellet of earth.

"Wait! " the sergeant ordered.

He jumped into the grave, took the flag off Corriveau's coffin, and climbed out.

"Now you can go . . ."

The gravedigger hastily filled in the hole with snow and earth.

The priest in his long black cope threw holy water, which didn't take long to freeze.

★ ★ ★ ★ ★

For Bérubé it was not over yet. The sergeant ordered him to find a carpenter in the village who knew how to make a coffin.

112

Bérubé returned in the afternoon with a roughly made coffin. The Anglais Henri had killed was laid in it. The coffin was covered with Corriveau's flag.

Bérubé realized that his punishment was finally going to begin.

The sergeant ordered him to carry the Anglais' coffin with the other soldiers.

Without speaking, they carried away the body of the hero killed while he was doing his duty.

Molly walked behind them. Because of her white gown, she was the first to disappear.

★ ★ ★ ★ ★

The war had dirtied the snow.

HOUSE OF ANANSI FICTION